MANIFESTO

SAUL WARSHAW

Cover Design by Danielle Stamper

Full Moon Publishing, LLC
Glade Spring, VA
Fullmoonpublishingllc.com

ISBN: 1946232025
ISBN-13: 978-1946232021

CONTENTS

PROLOG....1973

"They're dead," he said. "They killed them."
Sadness and anger were intermingled in his voice.
"My three sons. My wife.
"What can I do?
"What can I do now? For our family?

CHAPTER ONE
THE YEAR....2002

Until seven years ago, I was a homicide detective with the Los Angeles Police Department. Then, after my thirty on the Job, I retired and opened my agency, Will Jonas Investigations.

That's thirty-seven years of dealing with this thing called – "Crime," and the people who generate it. Plenty of odd cases in that mix. And now, as I drove on Winnetka, toward the Northridge LAPD Station on Devonshire in the San Fernando Valley, it looked like I was about to get involved in another odd one.

Someone had come to the Station and predicted the upcoming death – to be more precise – the murder – of a high level public official. Possibly one of the 15 members of the Los Angeles City Council, he claimed. Although he thought the victim might not be on the Council – and instead, be a career civil servant, or even a California state elected official or bureaucrat.

Now, whatever you think about these officials, when someone says one of them is going to be killed – you have to pay attention, right? You have to get involved. And that's what I was about to do, after getting a phone call from Charlie Black, my former partner in homicide and still with the LAPD.

Charlie said that Captain Klinger, head of the Northridge Station, wanted to talk to me about the person who was making the prediction.

A word about Captain Klinger.

When I was still on the job, Klinger and I did not get along. The Captain was a by-the-book operator. I am not.

Charlie and I, as a team, also were not. Our view was, what will it take to get this obviously guilty slob into the prison system for a long time? And if a few rules got bent along the way...

Can you see the conflict here?

I arrived at the station, parked in back, walked around to the front entrance, and went in. Charlie was waiting for me.

When we were partners, Charlie always played the "good

cop," while I was the "bad" one. Easy enough to see why. Charlie was 5 feet nine inches, and weighed a well-rounded – and I do mean, well-rounded – 195 pounds.

I'm six feet four, weigh 210, and at age 58, I'm still in pretty good shape.

What Charlie lacks in buff, though, he makes up in brains. One of the smartest people I know.

"Ready for this one?" Charlie greeted me.

"Who's going to die?"

"That's for you to find out."

Charlie nodded toward the back of the station.

"Come on. Klinger's waiting for us."

I followed Charlie to the double doors of a small conference room. I knew the room. We used to hold press conferences in it.

Klinger was waiting, sitting at the head of the table. He stood, and we shook hands.

"Will," Klinger said. "Thank you for coming in, on such short notice."

His voice was friendly, no sign of the usual tension he and I used to feel toward each other, so I played it the same way.

"Couldn't keep me away, Captain, once Charlie explained what this was about."

"Yes, it is a little different."

We sat down, and Klinger slid a manila file folder over to me.

I opened it and saw a head shot of a man.

"That's Roswell Clarence Bridgeman," Klinger said, "The reason for this meeting."

I asked, "And he's the one predicting the killing of an official here? Maybe one of our city councilmen, right? Or, I guess I should say...council persons?"

See? I'm right up there, when it comes to being politically correct.

"He's the one," Klinger confirmed.

"And why is anyone paying attention to what he's saying?"

"Because the same thing happened four years ago. In 1998. In Helena, Montana. Bridgeman predicted a high up official was going to be killed. And a few weeks later, the head of the Department of Sanitation was murdered. Shot in the head. Sitting in his car. In a restaurant parking lot."

2

"Did Bridgeman predict that specific guy's death?" I asked.

"No," Charlie got into the conversation. "Just that someone was going to be killed."

"Bridgeman was investigated, of course?" I asked.

"Number one suspect." Charlie confirmed. "But he had a pretty good alibi. And they could never prove anything.

"So, did they ever solve it?"

"Not as of an hour ago," Klinger said, "When I checked with Chief Halley, Helena Police Department. "

I looked at Bridgeman's picture. Definitely not a smiler. Just the opposite. Not a guy you'd want to share a beer with. But who knows? What can you tell from a picture?

Charlie interrupted my thought.

"You'll get to meet him as soon as we're finished, Will. And yes, he's the type who takes things seriously."

Charlie knows me so well. He could tell what I was thinking.

"Captain," I said, "I appreciate being called in, but why me? I mean, this is potentially a big deal. Especially if the media get on to it. Isn't this something that should be handled downtown? By Major Crimes? Maybe the homicide special people?"

"Yes and no," Klinger said. The Captain looked down at some notes, on a pad in front of him.

"Here's the thinking – and this comes from the top. The Mayor. The President of the City Council. And somewhat reluctantly, the Chief.

"First, despite what happened in Helena, who knows what gives with Bridgeman? I mean, do you believe in these people who go around making predictions like this? I don't. And the powers that be, are very skeptical as to what he is claiming.

"Second, even if Bridgeman is a solid citizen type, do we really want it known to the public – and the media – that someone is predicting the murder of a council member, or some other high level official? You know what *that* will turn into. Sick jokes and all.

"Third – yes, everyone agrees that we have to investigate this every-which-way-we-can. But quietly. Discreetly."

Klinger paused, then continued.

"But here's where it gets tricky, Will.

"Major Crimes downtown does not want to give up this

investigation. And they have enough clout, so that what they want, they're getting…sort of."

"Sort of?" I interrupted.

"They'll be heading up the investigation. But on a very inactive basis. They recognize that one of the problems with using their personnel, is that they are well known to the reporters who cover the crime beat, politics, city hall – you get the idea. Having their people nosing around, asking questions – well, there is concern about the media finding out what's happening. And then we'd have ourselves a circus.

"And that's where you come in. I suggested it might make sense to have someone like you – experienced, but not exactly a well-known LAPD face, anymore – do some of the initial legwork.

"And by legwork, I mean – get to know Bridgeman up close. Have him give you whatever details he can, about the supposed upcoming killing. See if it makes any sense – and if we should take it to a more serious level of investigation, action, personal protection for the council members. That sort of thing."

"All the while, I'd have Major Crimes breathing down my neck," I said.

Klinger nodded. "Yeah, Will. If you take this on, you're going to have that proverbial tiger by the tail. More specifically, Dan Foster, the lead detective on the Bridgeman investigation in the Crimes division of LAPD."

I didn't know Foster, but I figured he had to be a major force, if the Division was putting him up there, to shoot me down at the first chance they had. So they could take over the active part of the investigation. But what the hell. It wasn't like my job was at risk. Hey! I was retired from the Job. And on this one, they wanted *me*. So, full speed ahead, I said to myself.

While to Klinger, I said, "You told me Major Crimes would head this up – on a very inactive basis. What does that mean?"

"It means they'll get copies of all reports you file with Charlie and me. It means that if they feel, at any point, that you are screwing up, then they'll be after your head. But day to day, they won't be involved."

Klinger paused. "I guess I should also tell you that Foster does not like folks like you. Or to use his term – rent-a-cops."

Klinger took a moment to look again at his notes.

4

"I know this whole thing sounds very odd, Will. But there is Helena to consider. There, they kept things quiet. No media coverage of Bridgeman's prediction. In fact, they worked hard to keep the situation quiet. Mainly because they didn't take Bridgeman seriously. Then they had the homicide, and from the mayor on down, they're still getting criticized by the media and the public."

"Captain," I said, "I didn't have time to do any research, but don't these – what do you call them...psychics—usually claim to know where a victim's remains can be found? And isn't *that* how they try and help the police? *After* the homicide? Not *predicting* an upcoming murder?"

"That's right," Charlie answered my question. "But this one's what it is, Will. Bridgeman *is* predicting, and we've got to figure out how to handle it."

"So Los Angeles doesn't have a result like Helena," I said.

"Absolutely," Klinger said. "Get us the knowledge we need, Will. Get as much detail as you can. About what Bridgeman is claiming will happen. And who the victim will be. Take him all around the City. Hell! The State, if you think it will be useful.

I shook my head.

"Captain, I'll take this on," I said. "But it wouldn't surprise me if Bridgeman turned out to be a nutcase."

"Maybe," Klinger conceded. "But we have to play it out."

He checked his note pad.

"As for compensation, you'll be paid at your old grade level. That okay with you?"

This was more than okay.

"So, when do I get to meet this clairvoyant?" I asked.

Bet you didn't think I even knew that word, did you?

5

CHAPTER TWO

Nashville, Tenn....June 10, 1974

The body of Nashville Metropolitan Council member Merton Ogilvy was discovered late last night in Ogilvy's car, parked in the driveway of his home.

According to Nashville police, Ogilvy had been shot multiple times and was dead at the scene.

Councilman Ogilvy recently was acquitted of two counts of bribery, following a trial in which he was accused of accepting $40,000 in illegal campaign contributions. At the time, Ogilvy was serving on a special Council committee considering changes in the City's building code, which some have charged were favorable to real estate developers in the county.

CHAPTER THREE

Roswell Clarence Bridgeman was in a room, a few doors down from where Klinger, Charlie and I had met. He was seated at a small conference table, and he stood up as Charlie made the introductions.

"Mr. Bridgeman, this is Will Jonas, a special investigator with the Los Angeles Police Department. Will is going to be working directly with you, regarding what you've told us."

Bridgeman was tall. Almost as tall as me. He was thin, in a hard way – like tempered steel. A longish face, with slightly caved in cheeks. A mouth surrounded by thin, tight-to-the skin lips. Deep brown eyes that looked directly at me...and never seemed to blink. His hair was dark brown, thinning, with spots of gray throughout, and it looked like he'd gotten his last haircut at one of those student barber schools where they do it for nothing, so the students can get experience.

His clothes were right off the rack A pair of black all-purpose slacks. A gray casual shirt, buttoned all the way up. And a loose fitting, gray windbreaker.

Taken altogether, nothing particularly wrong with the guy, but not someone you'd especially want to meet in an alley one dark night.

"So you're shunting me off to some special sideshow, because you don't believe a word of what I'm telling you?" Bridgeman asked Charlie, his words forced out from between two almost immobile and definitely not smiling lips.

As he spoke, Bridgeman repeatedly clenched and unclenched his large hands. To me, a sure sign that he was feeling very uptight.

Time for me to defuse things!

"On the contrary," I said, walking up close to the man and extending my hand. "We're taking what you've told us very seriously. But we also don't want to panic any of the City Council members. Or other possible targets. And we certainly don't want to get the media involved. So the decision was made, the best way to work this, was to have someone give 100 per cent, 24-hour-a-day attention to what you are saying. And that someone is me."

I kept my hand extended, and after a few seconds, Bridgeman took it, and we shook.

Then, I took the seat next to Bridgeman and leaned in toward him, trying for some close, personal contact.

"Look, Mr. Bridgeman," I said, "We know it's taken a lot of guts on your part to come to us with your belief. And we respect that. And as I've said, we feel the best way to move forward is for you and me to work this hard – and together."

I paused, then leaned in even closer to the man.

"So, we good to go, Mr. Bridgeman? Because I want to start right now."

I stopped talking, smiled and nodded at Bridgeman, waiting for an answer.

My performance got an "A."

"All right," he agreed.

CHAPTER FOUR

With Bridgeman calmed down, Charlie left us, and I went to work.

"First off," I said, taking out my note pad, "I want to get some of your personal history."

About the pad – I didn't really need it. My memory is close to photographic. But I've noticed that most people, when I interview them, feel more comfortable when they see me writing down what they're saying.

"I gave all of that, already," Bridgeman's irritation level started to go up again.

I quickly flipped through the file. Saw one background sheet. Nothing in depth. Figured the Major Crimes guys didn't think much of Bridgeman's prediction, so they hadn't bothered to get the data. I wanted it. So I pushed.

"Of course," I agreed. "But if you don't mind, I'd like to get the information myself. Easier for me to absorb, and it will be more useful to me in our investigation."

I looked at the background sheet.

"According to this," I said, "You came to Los Angeles about a year ago. From Phoenix, Arizona."

"Correct."

"No family?"

"I'm a widower."

"Any children?"

"I said I'm a widower."

Not a man of many words, our Mr. Bridgeman. I ploughed on.

"You're working as a drug clerk in one of the "Best RX" drugstores. The one that's here in the valley, in Reseda, at Tampa and Sherman Way?"

"Yes."

"How long were you in Phoenix? And where'd you live before that?"

"Why is that important?" Bridgeman asked, the irritation again showing in his voice.

"Not that important in itself," I said soothingly. "Just want to get to know you a bit better. Always a good idea to get to know someone, when you're working with them, don't you agree?"

"Nada."

My explanation didn't really register with the guy. For whatever his reason, Bridgeman didn't want to give up any personal information. Well, me being me, that just made me more determined to get it. So I pushed.

"Trust me, Mr. Bridgeman. The more I know about you, the better a chance I have of helping you. And can I call you 'Ross'? Or 'Roswell'? Or what?"

"Ross will do."

"Thank you, Ross. And now back to my questions. How long did you live in Phoenix? And where did you live before that?"

In the silence that followed, I outlasted him, and he finally answered.

"I was in Phoenix for about nine months. Before that, I lived in Santa Fe, New Mexico."

"And in those places, did you also work for Best RX?"

"Yes," Bridgeman answered through tight lips.

Okay, I said to myself. Enough pushing for now. Let's come back to more comfortable territory.

"Ross, let's talk about Helena, Montana. According to the file, you made a similar prediction there, four years ago. And it came true. Right?"

"Yes."

"The head of the Department of Sanitation was shot and killed, correct?"

"That's right. He also had just been convicted of taking bribes from homeowners in the better part of town, to get their streets plowed first."

I shook my head.

"So the guy made money out of snow," I said. "Imaginative— even if illegal.

Bridgeman banged his fist down on the table.

"He was a convicted criminal! He did wrong! Can't you see the justice in what happened to him?"

I couldn't resist.

"Death for illegal snow removal? Kind of a harsh form of

10

justice."

Bridgeman didn't respond. Just sat there.

I switched topics.

"Any other places – besides Helena and Los Angeles — where you made predictions like this? Or maybe a little different? But predictions, nonetheless?"

"No. These are the only two."

"Ross, I've never worked with someone like you. Someone who predicts a homicide—and then it happens. So I need to know more about how you do it. How you think. What gives you the belief that something like this is going to *happen?* Like it did in Helena? And like you've said it's going to happen, here in Los Angeles?"

Bridgeman shrugged.

"*Why* I get these—these feelings? I don't know. I just—get them."

"Does something trigger them?"

I jerked a bit when I realized my choice of words. Using the word "trigger" in this discussion wasn't too sharp, but Bridgeman didn't seem to notice.

"The knowledge... just comes on. I get a feeling. Something important is going to happen. And then it comes to me. That someone is going to die. To be killed. And I get some information about the person. No names, though. No clear picture of the person."

I asked, "But both in Helena and here, you did get some information that the people were public officials. Right?"

"Yes."

"Anything more specific on that point? Maybe the particular position the person holds in government? Here in Los Angeles?"

"No. Just what I've given you. 'A high level government official.'"

"How did you get that feeling? That belief?" I asked.

Bridgeman shook his head.

"I can't tell you. It — it was just there. After I got my feeling about the official...well...It just seemed to me, that he was high level. That's just the way it was."

"You say... 'he.' Could it just as well be a 'she.'"?

Bridgeman thought about it.

"I guess it could be a 'she.'"

"Regarding what you've predicted for Los Angeles, is there any time line to your prediction? Anything telling you *when* this is going to happen?"

Bridgeman paused.

"I haven't said anything yet. To anyone. Because it's still not clear in my mind. But late yesterday, I started getting a feeling that it's going to happen soon."

"Soon?" I pushed. "Nothing any clearer? More specific?"

"No. Just...soon..."

"And you can't tell me anything more? What the person looks like? Man? Woman? Title?

"No. Nothing like that."

I studied Bridgeman's face.

He stared back at me – his face blank. No emotion. No anything.

This bugged me. It didn't make sense to me that someone telling us what he was telling us – well, he seemed too damn calm about the whole deal.

Not sure why. But I would have felt more comfortable, if Bridgeman were more obviously up tight. Troubled by the situation he had created.

And I began to wonder. Was Bridgman playing me? Playing all of us? For some reason not yet clear? But playing us, all the same?

Nah, I reasoned with myself. That doesn't make sense. What's the gain for Bridgeman in doing that? There isn't any. It's just that he's one serious dude. No humor in that body. Just deal with it, okay?

I thought about my next move.

"Tell you what," I said to Bridgeman, "I want to take you downtown. To City Hall. To give you a close up look at the place. And also, we can get a closer look at the council members. Let's see if that kind of proximity jogs any new facts out of you."

CHAPTER FIVE
The Year: 1986

Yes, we are serving the memory of our Family.

Our Family. Taken from us, by the corruption and the evil of those officials.

We search for this Evil.

We seek it.

And when we find it, we give this Evil what it deserves.

CHAPTER SIX

Meet the other member of my two-person Will Jonas Investigations agency—Rose Shapiro.

I describe Rose as my secretary-telephone operator-receptionist-bookkeeper-researcher-Jewish mother-person.

And Rose is all of that. This 60-plus, gray-hair-tied-in-back, short and round lady, marched into my office six years ago. Rose never walks, she marches, in those sensible, low healed, lace up shoes.

I'd spent the day interviewing air head ladies, looking for my first assistant. Rose was the last on the list, and when I looked at her, I wanted to ask why the hell she wasn't drinking tea, in her rocking chair at some senior citizen center.

But instead, Rose took charge of me. She told me I looked tired, she ordered me to sit down, and then she made me the best cup of coffee I'd had in almost four years, ever since my wife, Vera, had died.

I hired her on the spot – although I think she actually hired me.

Now, after I described the Bridgeman case to her, Rose asked, "So which one of our deserving politicians is going to get it?"

Then she waived her hand, apologetically.

"Sorry. Just joking. And I should know better. A novi is a serious matter."

Rose got me on that one. As she always does, when she pulls something Jewish on me.

"Okay," I said, "What's a novi?"

"It's a Hebrew word."

"That much I figured. But what does it mean?"

"It means...a prophet. Someone who can see into the future. At least in very general terms. There are several of them in a biblical collection called 'The Book of Prophets.'"

I shook my head.

"This guy...this Roswell Clarence Bridgeman...doesn't strike me as any prophet. In fact, I'm not at all sure he's legitimate. But my job is to check him out. And that's what we're going to do."

14

"And from me, what do you want?" Rose asked.

"I want you to use that computer magic of yours, and see what you can turn up, about Bridgeman. He didn't want to give me any personal details. And I have to wonder why.

"I got out of him that, before he came to Los Angeles, about a year ago, he was living in Phoenix, Arizona. And before that, in Santa Fe, New Mexico. And we do know that four years ago, he lived in Helena, Montana.

"So using those as your starting points, see if you can locate where else he's lived."

I looked at my notes.

"Yeah. And one more thing. See if you can find some information about psychics who are supposed to have helped police departments find the bodies of missing persons. Or if any of them have ever made any predictions about upcoming killings – and then those actually happened. Like in Helena."

CHAPTER SEVEN

Before I left the Northridge Station, I'd asked Klinger to call Chief Halley in Helena, Montana, and to ask the Chief to take a call from me. I wanted to talk to him about what had happened, there, with Bridgeman.

Halley had said okay, and now I dialed the number Klinger had given me. Turned out to be Halley's direct line. He answered it himself.

"This is Chief Mike Halley. Who's calling?"

I was surprised Halley wasn't screening his calls. Hey, he's the Chief of Police. But I reminded myself that Helena was one heck of a lot smaller than Los Angeles. Still sort of "small town" – I guess. And I mean that in a good way.

"Chief Halley, this is Will Jonas in Los Angeles. Captain Klinger called and asked that you take my call?"

"Yes, sir...so he did. Can't say I'm happy to get it. Anything that reminds me of what happened – well, it's not among my favorite memories."

"I can understand that."

"Hang on a second. I want to get Tom Voight in on this line. Tom was the lead detective on this case. He technically still is, of course, since the homicide isn't solved, so the case isn't closed."

There was a pause, then Halley came back, on a loudspeaker.

"Will Jonas, I'd like you to meet Tom Voight. Will, I've already filled Tom in, on what your assignment is with LAPD, with reference to Ross Bridgeman."

"Hey," Voight said, "Good to meet you, Will. And here's wishing you a lot better luck with your case, than we've had with ours."

"Well," I answered, "We are taking a closer look at the deal, than you folks did. But only because your case turned out the way it did. Otherwise, I'm sure that what Bridgeman is claiming is going to happen in Los Angeles, would be sitting at the bottom of some pile here."

"So, how can we help you?" Halley asked.

"I have some questions I'd like to ask you and Tom. Not so

16

much about the case. I've got a copy of your file, Tom. The one Chief Halley sent to our Major Crimes people. They passed it on to the guy I'm reporting to – Captain Klinger – and he's given it to me."

"So, how can we help you?" Tom asked.

"By giving me some information about Bridgeman, himself. What are your feelings about him? Your impressions about him? Is he believable?"

Voight laughed, but there was no humor in it.

"I guess I'd have to say, Bridgeman was very believable, here in Helena. I mean, the guy predicted what he predicted – and bam – that's what happened. But I know what you mean. And here's my feeling.

"He's an odd one. Very intense. Very tightly wound. Not a guy who tells jokes. Or laughs at them."

Chief Halley said, "I agree with Tom. There's no – I guess for want of a better word – no humanity in the guy."

I shifted gears.

"I understand you had Bridgeman as number one on your suspect list, after the killing. But you concluded that he wasn't the killer?"

Voight answered.

"The coroner estimated that Claude Fromin – that's the Department of Sanitation supervisor – was killed between 5 PM and 9 PM. Bridgeman was working at Best RX on a shift from 6 PM to midnight. So, yes, he did have a time slot to do the killing. That would be from 5 to 6 PM. But we could never find anything tying him to the scene. Nothing indicating he had ever met Fromin. No interactions at all between them. And that's as far as we ever got."

"And no one else ever turned up? As a possible killer? Someone maybe associated with Bridgeman?"

"Not that we could find," Chief Halley said."

"You know," Voight said, "I keep staring at the facts. And they are what they are. But I sure as hell still have a hard time accepting them. Some guy breezes into town. He's here for under a year. He predicts some official is going to get hit. It happens. And the man has an alibi."

"You make it sound like you think Bridgeman had an

accomplice." I said. "Someone who actually did the killing."

"We looked at that angle, every which way," Halley said. "But we could never find anyone who fit the description of an accomplice. Never could tie Bridgeman to anyone. No way. No how."

CHAPTER EIGHT

"Go home. It's time," Rose said to me, after I finished my call with Halley and Voight.

So home I went, to the other woman in my life...Lucy McClellan who, although she kept her own name, was dutifully and legally married to me. And had been, for three years.

Lucy was, in my opinion, an outstandingly attractive woman. She was tall. About five feet nine inches. She weighed in at a curvy 136 pounds. Her hair was a deep red – what else would it be, with a name like McClellan? And her angular face, with its high cheek bones and perfect nose, gave Lu the appearance of a model, much younger looking than her 43 years.

Was I prejudiced? You bet!

As she usually did, when she was home before me, Lucy met me in the hall of our condo in Tarzana, with my regular drink – club soda on the rocks. Yes. I'm a recovering alcoholic. No big deal, though. No daily wrestling with the demon. I'd been sober for almost seven years, and did not have much in the way of temptation. I was one of the luckier ones, I realized.

The club soda tasted refreshing. And dinner smelled even better.

"What's it going to be tonight?" I asked.

About six months ago, Lucy decided we were eating out too much.

"It's not just expensive," she said, "but it's not healthy. Too much in the way of calories. So I'm going to start cooking dinner at home – at least a few times a week."

"Great idea," I told Lucy, "except that up to now, about all I've ever seen you cook are hard boiled eggs."

I was not exaggerating. Lucy was not a kitchen person.

But she is someone who, once she makes up her mind – well – watch out. Whatever is involved, it's going to happen.

So, Lucy bought cookbooks, took classes, watched the cooking shows on tv – and what we have now, six months later – is a pretty accomplished cook, with me benefitting from her efforts. I have no complaints.

Lucy answered my question.

"Tonight?   I made something simple. Swordfish with broccoli."

The swordfish was moist and tender, and the broccoli was crisp and tasty.

Is life good, or what?

After dinner, Lucy listened as I described my day – a habit we'd grown into, over the years we've been married. Talking about an investigation was a good opportunity for me to review the key points, maybe see some new angles. And Lucy, sharp as she is, often was helpful in this regard. The lady was no slouch in the brains department. She was the top computer programmer in a large, multi-office bank headquartered in Glendale.

"Wow.   That's a tricky one," she said, after I finished describing the case.

"Yeah," I agreed. I sighed. "Somehow, I wish this was one of those deals, where I could ask you to feed the details into your computer, and what would come back, would be the name of the official who's going to be killed."

Lu sat silently for a moment.

"Hey," I said. "I wasn't really suggesting you do that."

Lucy didn't pay any attention to my comment. She had a look on her face that I knew well. It said, "Leave me alone. I'm thinking..."

So I shut up.

And after another minute or two, Lucy looked at me and smiled.

"You know, what you're suggesting isn't really outside the realm of possibility. We just need to feed in the right facts, and ask the computer to ID the most likely candidates who might be killed."

This one was going right over my head.

"But what do you mean, by 'the need to feed in the right facts'? Like what would a 'right fact' be, in a situation like this?"

"Let me explain it this way," Lucy said. "If your investigation turns up enough profile-type information about the potential victim – then that data is what we put in.

"Then, we program in profile information for as large a group of potential victims, as you want.   City Council members, of

20

course. Top level appointed officials. Top tier civil servants.

"Now, the computer would compare the profile type information against the profiles of the potential victims we've programmed in. And we'd get back a list of the most likely targets for killing."

I took a while to play back in my mind what Lu had just told me.

"Sonofabitch!" I said. "Is what you just said really possible? Or is it just you, the computer programmer, out there in 'what if' space somewhere?"

"Will," Lucy said, "What I've just described is possible. What's still needed, though, is the profile information about the intended victim."

"The information I don't yet have," I agreed.

I nodded.

"Yep. I see that. But what I don't see, is how the hell I'm going to get it."

"That part's up to you, My Love," Lucy said.

Then she did an exaggerated batting of her eyelashes.

"Will, I know I've given you some things to think about. And I do believe I deserve a reward. Don't you?"

"I agree," I said. "Got anything particular in mind?"

"Yes. Can you guess?"

I tried. And you know what? I was right.

CHAPTER NINE

Jefferson City, Missouri...April 6, 1988

The county-wide, seven-day search for William Glick, Budget Director for State Senator James Macklin, ended today, with the discovery of Glick's body in a shallow grave on a farmer's field, five miles south of Jefferson City.

Police at the scene would not confirm how Glick died, citing the need to await the results of an autopsy, scheduled for tomorrow morning. An informed source did report, however, that Glick had been shot multiple times.

CHAPTER TEN

The whole deal felt sort of...I don't know...maybe the word is... awkward.

The idea of taking Ross Bridgeman down to Los Angeles City Hall, so that he could see the members of the City Council up close? With the hope that maybe he would get some indication – some feeling – which council person might be a likely candidate for murder?

Well...

"Hi, Mr. Councilman. A moment of your time, to meet Ross Bridgeman, please? Now, Ross, is this council person a likely candidate to bite the dust?"

Okay, so I exaggerate. But isn't that really what our visit is all about? To see if Bridgeman's proximity to the Council members stirs anything up in him?

"The Council meets in public session, starting at 10:00 AM every Tuesday, Wednesday and Friday," I told Bridgeman. "Except for the first Friday of each month, when they meet in the Van Nuys City Hall, in the San Fernando Valley. Tomorrow being Wednesday, the Council will be holding its regular session, downtown, and we're going to attend it."

So there we were, the next morning, sitting in the public seats of the John Ferraro Council Chamber. The way the seating is set up, council persons face the audience during the public sessions.

For a meeting to be legitimate, there has to be a quorum of council members present – that means eight or more of the 15. I counted nine council members on hand, so they were good to go. And I made note of the six missing members, figuring I'd get Bridgeman close to them, physically, before we left the building.

I gave Bridgeman plenty of time to look at each council member. Watching him, looking at them, I didn't see him focus in on anyone.

I prodded him.

"So. Any one of them mean anything to you?"

Bridgeman shook his head.

"Nothing so far."

He looked at the list I'd given him – the names of the council persons, their districts and the committees they headed in their Council workings.

"The person who heads the Transportation Committee – Raymond Fleck – he's not here today, right?" he asked.

I scanned the members in attendance.

"That's right. Fleck isn't here today. Any particular reason that you've picked up on his absence?" I asked. "Could he be a person of interest to us?"

"No, no," Bridgeman said. I just noticed his name on the full list, but not on the list of today's attendees."

"If Fleck is of special interest," I persisted, "please let me know, and I'll find him and get us physically close to him. It won't be a problem. And he won't suspect anything."

"I said it wasn't important!" Bridgeman barked at me. "Stop pushing me!"

I stared at the man. Push him? Hell, I wanted to do more than that, with this guy who was making us all do odd things, because of his prediction. And not for the first time, did I doubt Bridgeman's prediction—Helena, Montana notwithstanding.

But I figured my flying off the handle wouldn't achieve much, so I dialed back my anger and took a more conciliatory tone.

"Okay, Ross, now that you've seen these nine members of the Council, it's time for you to see the other six members."

"How do we do that?" Bridgeman asked.

"While the Council holds its public meetings here on the third floor, they have their executive offices up on the next floor – the fourth floor. We're going there now, just to walk around. With any luck, you'll actually see those six members – or at the least, you'll be exposed to their offices, up close. Maybe that will jog something loose."

Having figured that our visit to the public meeting of the City Council would miss a few of its members, I'd asked Captain Klinger to get us a floor pass, so that Bridgeman and I could get on to the fourth floor and walk down and back up the corridor, connecting the Council members' offices. The captain had come through, so when the Council meeting ended, we went up to the fourth floor. Fortunately for us, the Council did not hold a closed, executive committee meeting after the public meeting – so it looked to me like all 15 of the Council members were in their offices. So Bridgeman, without looking conspicuous, was able to get a "feel" for each council member.

When we finished our swing around the City Council offices, I asked Bridgeman, "Did you feel anything promising?"

Bridgeman shook his head.

"No."

Then he looked at the building's office directory, posted next to the elevator bank.

"I don't see anything here for any department of building and safety. Doesn't Los Angeles have one?"

"Yes it does. Only it's not located here."

"Where is it?"

"Not too far away," I told him. On Sawtelle Boulevard. Want to go there?"

Bridgeman thought for a moment.

"No. I don't think there'll be anything there for me. I can't feel anything about that department."

"Then, why did you ask about it?" I asked.

"Just curiosity," Bridgeman said. He looked at his watch. "I've got to go to work. Can you take me to the pharmacy?"

I wasn't exactly wild about Bridgeman going back to work. Hell, we needed to keep going with our visits to different places.

But he insisted on going to the store. Go figure!

CHAPTER ELEVEN

Bridgeman and I had seen the L.A. City Council folks on Wednesday. No action, there.

Next, I decided to "expose" Bridgeman to other groupings of high level politicians – both elected and appointed. Not only at the City level, but at county and state levels in the L.A. area.

So for the next few days, we walked. We sat. We looked. Nothing.

The more we did, the more we grew discouraged.

Correct that – the more *I* grew discouraged.

"There has to be a better way," I complained to Charlie Black, when he and I met for an update session at the Northridge Station.

"I keep taking this guy all over the place. But nothing's happening!"

"Hey, Will – what did you expect to happen?"

"I don't know! But I was hoping that Bridgeman might show some hint of something. Of anything. Like yeah, this could be a possibility. Or maybe that guy's got me interested. But nothing like that is happening."

I paused, and then continued.

"And something's really beginning to bug me, Charlie."

"And what's that?"

"I'm beginning to wonder if Bridgeman is just plain nuts. Yeah, maybe he does have some vision that's telling *him* that a high level person in L.A. is going to get hit. But so what? It could just be something his screwed up mind is thinking."

"But what about what happened in Helena?" Charlie asked. "He made his prediction there – and then there was a homicide."

"Maybe he just got lucky. By comparison to L.A., Helena's a small city. About 29,000 people in the area. Bridgeman went to the media, when the police were trying to keep things quiet. And the media gave his prediction a lot of coverage. So I'm thinking — maybe someone had a score to settle with the guy who got hit? And that someone used the coverage to do the dirty deed?

"In other words", Charlie picked up on my comment, "It was a murder that took advantage of the prediction. The attention stayed fixed on Bridgeman. And not on the guy who actually did

26

the killing."

"Exactly!" I confirmed.

"Okay," Charlie said, "I'll give you that possibility."

He thought for a moment.

"But so what, Will? What does that do for you, on this case? Where are you going to go with all of this? What's next?"

I shrugged, then grinned.

"Damned if I know, Charlie. I guess I'll just have to keep pushing, and see what happens."

CHAPTER TWELVE

Roswell Clarence Bridgeman sat in the tiny kitchen of his rented apartment on Variel Street in Chatsworth, and reviewed the literature he had gathered at the places he and Will Jonas had visited during the past several days.

Good material. Helpful, as he sought to confirm his decisions.

Los Angeles. The final focus of his journey.

Bridgeman frowned, as he thought about the fact that the Los Angeles police had decided not to publicize his prediction. He wanted that publicity. Just like he had wanted it in Helena.

Well, he thought, if they don't tell the media soon, then I will make a few calls, myself. Mention Helena, and that should take care of it.

CHAPTER THIRTEEN

"Doesn't look to me like you're getting anywhere with this Bridgeman," Dan Foster said to me.

We were in a small meeting room at Major Crimes, downtown. Foster had summoned me there, by calling Charlie, earlier in the day, and telling him he wanted to see me. His place. His timing.

Got the power picture here? Foster pulling rank – reminding us that he and Major Crimes were in charge. And that I – Rent-a-Cop, didn't count. So he wasn't going to call me to a meeting – he'd have Charlie send me the message.

"Will," Charlie had warned me – "don't turn this into a pissing match with Foster. Yeah, you can probably beat him in an arm wrestle –but you'd lose the investigation. Remember that."

As usual, Charlie was right. So I dialed back my dislike for the guy and tried to sound cooperative when I answered him.

"I think we're making some progress, Dan. True, he doesn't seem to be getting closer to feeling any particular person might be the target. But on the other hand, he's physically gotten close to many potential targets – and none of them have turned him on. And that could be a good sign."

Foster shook his head.

"Nah. I don't see it that way. You're dragging him around town? What the hell is that accomplishing? Just using up gas and rubber, is what I think."

"Well, Dan, we're open to suggestions. What do you have in mind?"

"What do I have in mind? I'd drop the whole deal. I'd stop with the kid gloves. And I'd tell Bridgeman to either shut up with his predictions – or move to the next town. Get the hell out of Los Angeles."

"Sorry. But that's not going to happen. At least, not yet."

We stared at each other. Sort of a civilized arm wrestle, you might say. Then, hearing Charlie's warning in my mind, I tried to get the discussion back to something useful.

"One theory we're looking at is – maybe he's just plain nuts. You know, someone who imagines stuff like this."

Foster nodded.

"You do any testing on him? Any psychological studies?"

"Not yet. I don't think he'd go for it, so I haven't push it."

"Hell, I would. I'd push him hard. Get this thing settled. If we were running the investigation..."

Foster stopped short. His own words flapping in his face, telling him the obvious – "you're not really in charge. This rent-a-cop sitting in front of you – he's running things."

Foster stood up.

"Got to go. You still remember the way out?"

I could have said something nasty at that point. But hearing Charlie's warning in my mind, I left, and used the men's room to win that particular match. At least I think I won...

CHAPTER FOURTEEN

Topeka, Kansas...February 12, 1996

The body of William Spielman, a prominent Topeka attorney, was found this morning, by his secretary, Clarice Snyder, when she arrived at Spielman's office at 8:45 AM. He had been shot multiple times, a police spokesman said.

Spielman, a well-known defense attorney, last represented Ronald Glazer, who was charged with the death of his wife, Geraldine, after she had sued for divorce and accused Glazer of stealing two million dollars from a jointly held bank account. On January 9th, Glazer was acquitted of all charges.

CHAPTER FIFTEEN

"How'd the meeting go with Foster?" Charlie asked me, later that day, when I'd come back to the Station in Chatsworth.

"About like you'd expect. Short and unfriendly. Foster kept running into the fact that – even though, on paper, he's in charge -- he isn't really in charge."

"But if he *was* in charge? Did he tell you what he would do?"

"He said he'd push Bridgeman hard. Maybe get him psychologically tested. Probably end up figuring he was nuts, and run him out of town."

I shook my head.

"Charlie, you know something? Foster isn't one hundred per cent wrong in the way he's thinking."

"Explain."

I thought for a moment before answering.

"I'll put it this way. If I had come to L.A. – and made the prediction Bridgeman did make – and if, then, the police paid me the attention they are paying me – and they gave me my very own tour guide – that's me – to take me all over the damned city, to see if any useful, association-kind of stuff comes up – well – I'd show some excitement. Some involvement. Be thankful for the interest. Hell, I don't know! Show some emotion of some sort."

"You're not getting that?" Charlie asked.

"I'm getting nothing! The guy is cooperative. He comes with me, wherever I want to take him. He pays attention to whatever I say. But he never offers any opinions about anything. He never laughs. He never raises his voice. He is in complete control of himself. At all times.

I shook my head.

"It's like...well...like he's got his own agenda. And he's just using us to further it. Like we're a set of tools in some grand plan that he's building."

"What kind of grand plan?" Charlie asked.

I took a deep breath as I worked through what I wanted to say. Because what I was thinking, was definitely way out there.

"Okay, let's start with this fact. Over the last few days,

Bridgeman's been asking me how come there is no publicity about his prediction? Why, as he put it – no media coverage?"

"You explained why, of course," Charlie said.

"Sure I did. But I'm telling you – he wants the coverage. I warned him to stay away from the media, but I can't guarantee that he will. Not unless you want to slap him into isolation in some hotel. And I'm sure you don't want to do that."

"Right," Charlie agreed.

"Okay, let's go some more. Think about the following.

"Somehow, in Helena, Bridgeman was successful in predicting the murder of that official. That head of their Department of Sanitation.

"How the hell he pulled that off – I don't know.

"But I do know this. I don't believe anyone – anyone – can predict a murder, like Bridgeman did in Helena, and then it happens."

"But it *did* happen, Will," Charlie interrupted.

I waved away what Charlie said, as I answered him.

"Yeah, it did happen. And in my book, that means one of two things. Either Bridgeman lucked out because that murder happened, and it made his prediction come true."

I paused for emphasis.

"Or – *he* did the dirty deed himself. *He* murdered that official. And the publicity he had generated, acted like a shield. It kept the suspicion off of him."

"Two things wrong with what you're thinking," Charlie said.

"First, *because* of the publicity, attention *was* on him. And second, he was investigated, and cleared.

I stared at Charlie.

"Wouldn't be the first time someone got away with murder," I said.

Charlie thought about it.

"Okay, Will. I'll give you that."

He nodded to himself as he reviewed what he wanted to say next.

"But...if what you're saying is true – then this means Bridgeman is planning to commit a murder here in Los Angeles."

"Right," I answer. "And what we're doing with him now – what *I'm* doing with him, is giving him all these close-up looks at the top level officials of the City, the County, even the State officials who are located here."

"So, maybe you should stop taking him around."

"Too late for that. I've pretty much taken him everywhere."

Charlie thought for a short while.

"So, then, what's your next step?"

"Steps – actually," I answered.

"First, I keep going around with him. There are a few places I can show him. Not first choice stuff – but I want to keep him going. I want to keep watching him, and trying to figure him out.

"Second, I want to start seeing what I can find in his background. He seems to drift from city to city. I want to get more information about that.

"And third, I want to hop up to Helena. Want to talk some more with Chief Halley and his lead detective, Tom Voight. And also to the writer who covered the story for the local paper, the Helena Independent Record. Try to learn more about Bridgeman."

CHAPTER SIXTEEN

"Don't know what more you're going to learn, by coming up here," Tom Voight said, when I called him later that day, after getting back to my office."

"Not sure, myself, Tom," I told him. "But I just got a feeling I may pick up something. Maybe with you. Maybe with that reporter, Ben Franks."

"Have you spoken to Franks yet?"

"No. I wanted to talk to you, first."

"Glad you did.

There was a pause in the conversation, until Voight talked again.

"Franks is a good guy. A good reporter. A fair one, too. But he's a reporter. He makes his living finding out things and writing about them. So, I'm wondering if you realize what could happen, once he finds out who you're talking about."

"You mean, he'd call one of his contacts at the Los Angeles Times and tip him off to this story? Or, go after it himself. And there goes our effort to keep this out of the media?"

"Exactly."

"I think I can handle that, Tom. If Franks is like most good reporters, and he smells a big story around the corner – but only if he'll cooperate and stay silent for a while – well, I think I can convince him on that point."

"Good luck with that."

"Thanks. Is tomorrow okay for me to fly up and meet with you? And then I'll try and see Franks, after that."

"Works for me, Will. Looking forward to meeting you."

CHAPTER SEVENTEEN

After talking with Tom Voight, I called Rose into my office.

"Need you to book me a reservation. Want to fly up to Helena, Montana tomorrow morning. And then fly back in the evening. Burbank Airport would be nice, but LAX if necessary."

"Will do," Rose said.

"How are you coming on that research I asked you to do?"

Rose handed me a file folder.

"Plenty of information about psychics and their work with police and other law enforcement services. But it's all on their trying to help the police find the victims."

"In other words," I said, "Aside from Bridgeman in Helena, there are no records of psychics or seers, or whatever you want to call them, predicting a murder, which then did happen?" I asked.

"That's right," Rose answered.

"I'm not surprised."

Rose questioned me.

"You don't think Bridgeman is kosher?"

"Not as kosher as your kitchen," I teased her.

I changed subjects.

"How about that research you were doing on Bridgeman? In those cities where he lived, before coming here to Los Angeles? Phoenix, Santa Fe, Helena. What did you turn up?"

Rose sighed as only Rose could sigh. So I knew the news wasn't good.

"This is a problem," she said. "It was hard to find any trace of him. Why? Because he didn't buy or sell any property – so no property taxes. He didn't own a car, so no vehicle registration. Or even a driver's license. He didn't get involved with any city agencies for anything. And, he wasn't registered to vote."

"It looks to me like he was trying to be invisible," I said. "Or at least, not be noticed."

"That's the feeling I get," Rose agreed.

"Okay, drop that one," I told her. "Let me think some more about what to do."

CHAPTER EIGHTEEN

The "what to do" came to me, as I was going home that evening.

So, after dinner – another gourmet achievement by Lucy – or as she described it – "Baby lamb chops, tender, and with just a tinge of pink," I raised the subject as we drank our coffee.

"I think I have a problem that you – with your computer savvy – can solve for me," I said.

"And that would be...?"

"I want to learn more about someone. Specifically, what he was doing as he lived in several cities. I gave Rose the list of cities, but she couldn't find any trace of the man. No real estate owned. No car owned. No driver's license. No voter registration. But, the man told me lived in those cities where Rose did her search."

"You're talking about that Bridgeman person, right?"

"Yes."

Lucy thought for a moment.

"In those cities, do you happen to know where he worked?"

"Well, here in Los Angeles, he's working as a drug clerk in one of the Best RX drugstores. Maybe he worked for them in the other cities? Can't be sure. But it's worth a try."

"Okay," Lucy said. "I'll see what I can find out."

And here, Folks, is where this chapter will end. Because Lu knew. And I knew. And you probably know – that Lu is intending to hack her way on to the Best RX personnel file. A "no-no?" Yep. But, what's that saying? "Justice will be served?"

CHAPTER NINETEEN

Well, I'm the one who decided to go to Helena, Montana. To interview the police and the newspaper reporter who covered the story four years ago, when Bridgeman predicted the murder of that local official, and as they say in the bible, "It came to pass..."

I thought it would be a quick and easy trip.

Like hopping from L.A. to San Francisco. Or to San Diego.

Wrong!

So, here I am, at 6:30 in the morning, eating breakfast aboard Alaska Airlines, on the way to Missoula, Montana. No direct flights to Helena, it turns out. We were due to land at noon in Missoula, and then I had a two-hour drive in a rental, to Helena.

Chief Halley and Detective Voight had agreed to see me in the afternoon. And I was having dinner with Ben Franks, the reporter for the Helena Independent Record. Then, I was scheduled to fly back the next morning.

I arrived at police headquarters just a little past 2 PM, and after a short wait, Tom Voight came out to meet me.

"Welcome to Helena and Montana, Will," he greeted me.

He shook his head.

"Sure hope you learn something useful. Heck of a trip to get here and back, huh? Like we are in the middle of nowhere."

"But a beautiful middle of nowhere," I said. "I enjoyed the drive from Missoula."

"Yeah, well – you had to say that. Now, let's go on back to the Chief's office," Tom said, starting down a hallway that led out of the reception area.

Halley's office was at the end of the hallway. As Numero Uno offices go, it was a fair sized one. Nicely furnished, but not in the kind of rough wood finish furniture you'd expect. Instead, Halley went for more "office modern" digs. Steel and glass stuff.

A nice brag wall, showing the Chief with what I figured were the local and state Top Folk. And on his desk, three family pictures – a shot of Halley, his wife and two kids, nicely split between a boy and girl – a photo of the two children —and a close-up of Halley and his wife.

Chief Halley was 52 years old, I knew from my background reading. When he stood to meet me, I saw he was about 5'-9" or 5'-10", compactly and trimly built. His hair was thinning a bit in front, and was a combination of brown, with some silver starting to get in the mix.

Tom Voight was considerably younger – I figured him for the mid-30's. He was almost as tall as me, and he was built on the lean side. His hair was still its original black. No evidence of any grey coming on.

Halley came around from behind his desk and led us to a small sitting area. He took the only chair and Tom and I sat on the couch.

After we talked about the trip a bit, the getting-from-there-to-here difficulties, Tom asked the first question.

"So, what do you want to know, Will?" he asked. "How can we help you?"

"What I mainly want to concentrate on," I answered, "are not the details about the killing. Your file is solid and it doesn't leave me with many questions.

"What I'm really looking for, is anything you can tell me about Ross Bridgeman. He's been one tight lipped guy with me. Even had a hard time, getting him to tell me where he'd lived before coming to Los Angeles. Or before he came to you, in Helena. It's to the point where I'm wondering what's going on with this guy? Is he just maybe – well, nuts –with these predictions of his? Or does he have some sort of a plan for what he's doing? Something he wants to achieve, but he doesn't want anyone to know what that plan is."

I looked at the Chief and at Voight.

"Does what I'm saying make any sense to you? Or am I way off base, here?

Chief Halley shook his head.

"No, you're right on. Bridgeman *was* one close mouthed fella. Didn't want to give out too many details about himself. Which of course struck me as odd, seeing as he'd come to us. Looking for us to pay attention to what he had to say."

"In our case," Voight picked up on the discussion, "We didn't pay much attention to what he was saying, because as you know, we didn't really believe him. We decided he was just some nut case from somewhere, and if we didn't give him any attention, then chances were, he'd move on."

"Didn't turn out that way, of course," Halley muttered. "Much to our eternal regret."

"But when you *did* get to know him better, after the murder, and you were considering him as a suspect, did he open up to you? Did you learn any more about the guy?"

Voight shook his head.

"Not much." he said.

"But like you, I got the impression Bridgeman had something specific in mind. Something beyond what was happening, here in Helena. Like you said, it was as if he had some plan he was following."

"Tom and I talked about this a lot," Haller said. "We both had that same feeling. And we questioned Bridgeman along the lines of "what are you doing here? Why did you come to Helena? Stuff like that."

"But we never got much out of him," Tom added.

"What about family?" I asked. "He told me he was a long time widower. But again, no details. Nothing about family, wife, kids."

"We drew a blank on that one. We knew he had come to Helena from Lincoln, Nebraska. But we didn't get much there, either. He just said he had spent about a year there."

I made a note in my file, while explaining to Haller and Voight, that "Lincoln is a new city for me. Not on my list of where Bridgeman told me he'd been."

Our discussion went on a while longer, but nothing new or useful came up. So, we ended the meeting, and Tom offered to drive me over to the Howard Johnson's Inn, where I was registered for the night.

Would I have liked to stay at the Residence Inn or the Best Western, both more upscale? Sure. But I'd had a hard time getting Klinger to agree to the trip and its cost. So I'd settled for the much lower room cost Howard Johnson's – which turned out to be just fine. Another plus was that their dining room stayed open until 10 PM, not a mean achievement in a comparatively small town of 29,000 people, give or take a few thousand.

CHAPTER TWENTY

Once I'd checked in, I called Ben Franks at the Independent Record and confirmed that he'd be meeting me for dinner. I told him to call my room, when he got to the hotel, and I'd meet him at the entrance to the restaurant.

Then I took a quick shower and checked the time. It was 6:45 local time, meaning 5:45 in Los Angeles. I figured Charlie might still be at his desk, so I called him.

But before we go any further, I want to let you know that I made that call on my new cell phone. A few weeks ago, Lu leased the phone for me, over my protest. The damn thing scared me, what with all the stuff it could do. I would have been happier just to pick up the phone on the night table and make the call.

But progress needs to be served, right? That's the way Lu put it to me, so what else could I do?

"Detective Black," Charlie answered.

"It's me...Will."

"Ah, the Detective of the Plains. How's your horse?"

"Enough with the jokes. What's going on there?"

"You mean with Bridgeman?" Charlie asked. "Actually, he was over here today. Looking for you."

"Looking for me?"

"Indeed he was." Charlie's voice now turned serious.

"He wanted to know – actually, he demanded to know – why you weren't taking him around to see more places today. I explained that you were out of town, but that you'd be back tomorrow, and I was sure you had a full day planned for him."

"Interesting," I said, "That he's pushing so hard now. Wonder if that means he thinks something is about to happen."

"You mean the killing he's predicted, of course."

"One and the same."

"Hey! I thought you didn't believe him and his prediction at all! What? Are you changing your mind, Will?"

"Charlie, I'm not sure what I believe. On one side of it, I really don't believe him. But here I am in Helena, where it did happen. And so far, I haven't heard anything to shake the connection between his prediction and the murder of that guy – what was his name – Claude Fromin."

"So you didn't learn anything new, in your meeting with the chief and his detective?"

"Nada. Except, that they didn't get much more out of him that we've gotten so far."

"And tonight, you're seeing the reporter?"

"Yup. In about an hour."

"What time are you getting back tomorrow?"

"We land at LAX at 10:18 AM. I'll go straight to my office. Then I'll call Bridgeman and set up to meet him, for more touring."

"See you tomorrow," Charlie signed off.

Next up, I called Lucy, at our condo. Hoped she'd be there by then – it was now 6:00 pm in Los Angeles.

And she was.

So I panted.

But she wasn't fooled.

"Did I tell you," she began, "that one of the special features of that phone I bought you, is that if the caller pants or does anything else unusual, the caller's name comes up on my screen? Did I tell you that?"

"No, you didn't. And I don't believe you."

"Ah well, it was worth a try. And so, Will, My Love, how are you? And how are things going?

"I'm fine. I miss you. And nothing much is going."

"Meaning, nothing new uncovered?"

"Yup. Except for one item. Thanks to the folks here, I learned about another city, where Bridgeman lived, before ending up in Los Angeles."

"And that would be...?"

"Lincoln, Nebraska."

"Okay, I'll add it to the list."

There was a pause, and then Lu spoke again.

"Will, it's slow going – on what you asked me to do. That company – Best RX -- has a good system in place, to discourage hacking. I'll figure it out, eventually, but it's going to take more time."

CHAPTER TWENTY-ONE

At a few minutes before eight, the hotel phone rang in my room. It was Ben Franks, the reporter, letting me know that he was waiting outside the entrance to the restaurant.

I went down to meet him.

Franks looked to be in his late twenties, maybe early thirties. He held himself up straight, like many short people do, in an attempt to add as much height as he could to his frame. I estimated this brought him to about 5 feet 8 or 9 inches. Well built. Looked like he worked out regularly in the weight room. Full head of brown hair. Basic haircut –nothing fancy or special. He had a friendly, nice looking face, and a smile. Seemed like a regular guy, but I had to warn myself that he was a reporter, and his open and friendly manner probably was just his normal way of operating in interview and fact finding situations.

We shook hands and went into the restaurant, where we had our choice of tables. Not the gourmet attraction in Helena was the Howard Johnson's eatery. But it would serve both of our purposes.

"I have to say that it was hard for me to keep quiet about this meeting," Franks started right in. "I wanted to call one of my contacts at the L.A. Times, but I didn't – just as you asked."

"Thank you for that," I said. "Especially since I doubt if anyone at the Times would even know what you were talking about."

Franks laughed. "Yeah, I sort of got that impression when I went on line and couldn't find any stories about Bridgeman in any of the Los Angeles media – print, electronic, social—you name it."

Franks leaned across the table and stared at me.

"What I *did* find, though, was a lot of stuff on you. Big time, LAPD homicide detective. But – you retired seven years ago."

Franks gave me a double-take look.

"So what's going on, Jonas? Nothing about Bridgeman in the L.A. media. You, an ex-homicide detective, running some investigation for the LAPD. And you want to talk to me about Bridgeman and what happened here, four years ago. Before we

43

take this any further, it's time for some information. An explanation."

I didn't answer right away, on purpose. Wanted the tension to build up. Then I began.

"How old are you, Ben?"

My question threw him for a few seconds. Then he answered.

"Thirty -wo."

"How many years have you been here in Helena, with the Independent Record?"

"Six."

I paused again, for emphasis.

"Six years. You're thirty-two. I get the feeling you're ready to move into a bigger market. Maybe Denver or San Francisco. Am I right, Ben? Am I thinking along the right lines?"

Franks looked at me, then he nodded. Like he was admitting I was right – but he was afraid to say anything more, until he knew where I was going.

"Okay, Ben," I said. "I'm going to take a chance with you. I'm going to tell you some things that can turn into a helluva story – for you. One that can be your one-way ticket out of here, and up to a major market. But it's a story you can't run with yet."

"Why? Because it's only just now taking shape. And there's a chance it may never actually *take* shape. Because I'm working on some suspicions I have – about Ross Bridgeman — rather than any hard facts.

"However – and this is important -- if my suspicions do turn into facts, then – in addition to you having the story – we may be able to save someone from being murdered in Los Angeles."

I paused, for emphasis.

"And we may be able to solve the murder of Claude Fromin, here in Helena."

I stopped for a few seconds, then asked, "Okay, Ben. Are you ready to be the reporter who breaks this story? Who keeps getting the inside data from me, as the case moves along? Are you ready for that?"

Franks didn't answer me at once. He was having an internal wrestling match between his personal ambitions and his professional ethics as a reporter.

Then, he asked, "You say, there's no story yet, but that it'll be a big one, if/when it happens? And you say you want me to keep quiet now, so I can have an exclusive – as well as continuing inside stuff -- once the story breaks?"

"Correct."

Franks thought some more.

"One thing puzzles me. Why are you coming to me, now? If you hadn't called me – if we weren't meeting here now – I wouldn't be giving any thought to Bridgeman and that murder here, four years ago. So, why are you coming to me, now? Four years after the fact?"

"Because *now* is when I have to deal with Bridgeman in Los Angeles. He's come to us with the same story he came to Helena with. A prediction of a murder of a prominent local government official. And it's my job to try and figure out what is happening. And the more I get into it, the more I get suspicious about Bridgeman. Who is this guy? What's he really up to, with this prediction stuff? Despite our trying, he doesn't give up much in the way of personal information.

"So, I figured that since you wrote all those stories about Bridgeman, four years ago, you'd know more than I know. I want to pump you for all that you learned about the guy. I want to get to know all I can about him. So I can better deal with him in Los Angeles. So I can decide if he's a nutcase. Or if he's got some kind of a scam going with this murder prediction stuff he's coming up with. Or, if there is something else going on here."

I paused for emphasis.

"Like maybe…murder."

"Hey," Franks pointed out, "that 'prediction stuff,' as you call it – did happen here in Helena. Bridgeman did predict a murder. There was one. And Bridgeman was cleared of having anything to do with it."

I shook my head.

"That's all true. But there's something about the guy that is…off. He's keeping something hidden. Won't talk about his background. Won't really talk about anything. Too much there, we don't know. And I want to find out."

Franks stayed silent. He looked down at the table. He picked up his fork and played with it. He put down the fork. He looked at me.

"The thing is," he said, "Can I trust you?"

"The thing is," I answered, "Can I trust *you*?

We stared at each other. I decided it was now or never.

"I'm ready, right here and now, to give you everything we have, so you can begin to build your file. I'm ready."

I paused.

"Are you?"

I held my hand out.

Franks looked at it. He looked at me. Then he extended his hand, and we shook.

For the next hour, I asked Franks several questions. Bridgeman hadn't opened up much to the reporter, but he did give up some information that I didn't have.

Fact: Bridgeman had been a widower for 25 years, by the time he was living in Helena in 1998.

Fact: Bridgeman was a loner. Had no friends in Helena. And according to his co-workers at Best RX, he rejected any invitations to become friendly.

Fact: Bridgeman did not seem to have any accomplice who might have helped him kill Fromin, if indeed, he was responsible for that killing ("And he was cleared of it," Franks kept reminding me).

Fact: Bridgeman did seek out the publicity when he came to Helena and predicted an upcoming killing. It was clear to Franks that Bridgeman did want that coverage.

Fact: Bridgeman never expressed opinions about anything, with one exception. He disliked government officials.

We ended our meeting with Franks promising me that he'd review his files and notes that he'd saved, and let me know if he found any more information that he thought might be useful to me.

I promised him that I'd periodically update him on what was happening with Bridgeman in Los Angeles.

CHAPTER TWENTY-TWO

The next morning, after landing at LAX, I went to my office, where Ross Bridgeman was waiting for me. I knew he'd be there because Rose had alerted me, when I called in, from the airport.

"What can I tell you?" Rose asked, on the phone, and then she went on to answer her own question.

"He came in a little while ago. Wanted to know where you were. Nu? So I told him you were out. Period. That you would be back later. I didn't tell him anything else. He said he'd wait for you. He plopped himself down... and he's waiting."

I got to my office just before noon, and there was Ross, sitting in one of the visitor chairs in the small reception area.

"Good morning, Ross," I said, trying to keep my tone friendly. "Wasn't expecting to see you today. No visits are planned for today."

"Why is that?" Bridgeman demanded, the edginess clear in his voice. "Why no visits today? Why aren't you paying any attention to me, anymore?"

"We *are* paying attention," I countered. "We've been going out – almost every day. And we'll be going out again, very soon. Looking for anyone who might be a potential target."

"I don't think you're taking me seriously," Bridgeton came back at me, his tone aggressive.

"I don't understand what you mean."

Bridgeton leaned toward me for emphasis.

"What I mean is – there is no publicity about my prediction."

"We've been over all that," I said. "I explained our strategy to you. I thought you understood what we were doing."

"I understand. But I don't agree! And I'm ready to go to the press on my own!"

"I wouldn't do that, if I were you," I told him.

Bridgeman stared at me. I stared back. He broke first. Barely. Nothing said. But his body did sag, just a bit.

I said, trying mightily for a more friendly tone, "Listen, I'm going to set up more places to visit. I need tomorrow to make the arrangements. So we'll be going out again, day after tomorrow."

CHAPTER TWENTY-THREE

"Jonas! Jonas! Jonas!"

Ross Bridgeman ripped into the name as if it was a curse.

Seated at the small table in his kitchen, Bridgeman thought about Will Jonas, about the Los Angeles Police Department. And about his plans. What it was he intended to do. For oh such a long time.

Jonas was becoming a problem. He was always asking questions. Wanting to know about things he shouldn't know about.

Well, Jonas will be dealt with, at the right time. So that he would not stand in the way of what had to be done.

"Don't you see? He said aloud. "It is the culmination of my plans. What all the other punishings – over the years – have been building up to.

"Yes. It is my culmination."

CHAPTER TWENTY-FOUR

About 27 hours after Ross Bridgeman and I had our head-to-head in my office – his prediction came true.

A Los Angeles City Councilman was murdered.

The cause: five bullets from a .22, that penetrated the upper part of his chest. Actually, pretty good shooting. One .22 by itself probably would not have come close to being fatal. But five? That did it.

No mystery who did the shooting.

The councilman's wife — upset no doubt, by the sight of her beloved husband fully entwined with the willing body of his loyal secretary, in a motel on Sherman Way in Canoga Park.

Seems the wife had suspected her husband for some time, and had engaged the services of a private investigator, who called the lady to tell her that hubby, even as they spoke, was sharing a bed with the Other Woman at the Thrifty Inn.

Twenty minutes later, who shows up, but the Mrs. Not at all teary. No sobs from her. Instead, just rage, as she exited her car, carrying her husband's .22, which she knew he kept in the night table next to their bed.

She ran into the motel room occupied by her husband and his secretary – and a moment or two later, the Councilman's seat became eligible for a special election.

At that point, the new widow sank to the floor and started weeping, the Other Woman joined in the weeping for reasons of her own, and the private investigator called 911.

"Will, you better get out here," Charlie Black called to tell me. "The media's showing up like crazy. I figure Bridgeman will see the live tv coverage, and he'll probably come out here. And since he's so hot for publicity – well -- you know the rest."

CHAPTER TWENTY-FIVE

The Thrifty Inn was about a 20-minute ride from my office in Woodland Hills. Long enough for me to do some serious thinking. And out of that pondering, came some facts for me to consider.

First, while the "no publicity" policy might have been a good idea while we were still looking around for a possible victim – now that a candidate – the deceased councilman – had surfaced, Bridgeman would not be denied. He'd claim he predicted the killing, and he'd go for all the coverage he could get – and he'd get it.

Second, as far as I was concerned, no way did I figure that Bridgeman had foreseen the councilman's demise at the hands of his wife. That it happened that way, was just another lucky break for Bridgeman. Just like in Helena.

Third, could I prove any of this?

No.

But I just could not shake the feeling that Bridgeman was after something bigger.

But what?

I had no idea.

But the feeling persisted!

Well, okay, I decided. Let's give him all the publicity he can handle, and maybe it'll lead us somewhere useful.

But, I cautioned myself, I could not make it look like I was involved in generating any of the publicity. That would go down badly with Dan Foster and the Major Crimes folks.

I smiled. Well, I had this angle already covered, didn't I? Back in Helena, I'd worked things out with Ben Franks of the Independent Record. Now, I just had to get Luis Rivera, the Los Angeles Times crime beat reporter, into the deal.

Not to worry. Luis and I had worked together, many times over the years.

By now, I'd reached the Thrifty Inn.

End of thinking.

Time for action.

Police scene-of-crime tape blocked off the entrance to the motel's driveway. The press were clustered just to the right of the entrance, and as I'd hoped, I could see the Los Angeles Times' Luis Rivera heading the pack.

Luis and I went back many years. We'd cooperated on a regular basis, on various cases that Charlie Black and I were handling. I'd feed Luis some information that I wanted to go public, on a particular case.

Or I'd give Luis an angle on an investigation that none of the other media had. In return, Luis would weave into his coverage any particular points that I thought might be useful to the investigation.

When he spotted me – Luis held his hands out, and I hoped he was asking —"Will – what are you doing here? You're retired. What's the deal?"

I nodded at Luis, hoping he'd understand that I'd have something for him a bit later. And from his nod back, I knew he understood me.

What I intended to do, was to put Luis in touch with Ben Franks in Helena. By doing so, I'd come through on my promise to Franks, to get him involved in a bigger story. And Franks could give Luis information about the Helena case —specifically about Bridgeman and his prediction, there. And this would make the L.A. story even bigger.

Just what I wanted!

Charlie had left my name with the officer handling the entrance. I gave it to him, and after he checked his list, he waived me in. I went to the area where the other cars were, parked and followed the yellow tape over to the motel room.

"My name's Will Jonas," I told the uniform standing just outside the room. "Charlie Black told me to come out here."

The uniform nodded to another policeman who went into the room, and then he came back out, followed by Charlie, who took my elbow and guided me away from the room.

"Dan Foster is inside, telling Klinger that Major Crimes is going to take over the running of Ross Bridgeman, now that Bridgeman's prediction has come true. Foster's idea is to keep Bridgeman quiet about the prediction. The way he put it, he figures that if Bridgeman's prediction is known to the media, it'll turn into a circus. And he wants to avoid that."

"Foster is dreaming," I said. "Bridgeman wants the publicity. There is no way to keep him from approaching the media on his own. No way. And besides, I *want* him to talk to the press."

"Because you're still certain he's got something else planned for here in Los Angeles?"

"Yes I am."

"But this killing here tonight fulfills Bridgeman's prediction, doesn't it? So what makes you think there's more?"

"I don't have any hard facts, yet, Charlie. But I've gotten to know Bridgeman better than any of you – Foster included. And the reporter in Helena –Ben Franks –told me enough new stuff – so that I believe tonight's killing was just a lucky break for Bridgeman. Not anything he predicted. And that he has something else in mind, for his prediction."

"Well, I'm not convinced," Charlie said. "So, what are you going to do, to convince me?"

"I'm going to get things going, with two people. Luis Rivera of the Times. And Ben Franks of the Helena Independent Record."

CHAPTER TWENTY-SIX

Instead of going into the motel room – where I knew Foster would tell me I was off the case, I instead went back to my car and called Ben Franks. I figured he'd still be at the paper, putting the finish on whatever story he was working on for the next morning's edition.

"Ben Franks," he answered his phone.

"This is Will Jonas," I said, "And I'm calling to honor my promise to you."

"Okay!" Franks said, snapping to it, like any good reporter. "Tell me more!"

"To start with, Ross Bridgeman's prediction of a murder in Los Angeles just came true. Less than two hours ago. When a pissed off wife shot her husband, because he was in bed with his secretary. He – the deceased – was a Los Angeles City councilman. So that part also fits in with Bridgeman's prediction that the killing would involve a high elected or appointed official."

"Great L.A. story — but where does this do me any good?"

"The Los Angeles Times number one crime beat reporter is Luis Rivera. He and I have a long history of mutually beneficial cooperation. As soon as we hang up, I'm going to call Luis and tell him about Bridgeman in Helena, and about you. Luis will realize that his story will be that much bigger, with the Helena angle added to it. And I'll tell him you're willing to cooperate, to write the Helena part of the story – with byline credit to you. And that you're a guy who is ready for bigger than Helena. The rest is up to you, and how you can work with, and deal with, Luis."

"Fair enough. How do I reach him?"

"I'm going to give you his number. You wait about five minutes before calling him. I want to call him first, and tell him why he should talk to you."

"Okay."

"But one more thing, Ben. Don't use my name in anything you write. For what I'm going to be doing -- my name in any story is not a good thing. You clear on that?"

"I'm clear. What about Rivera?"

"I'll be telling him the same thing. He'll understand. He and I have done stuff together before."

I gave Rivera's number to Franks.

Then I called Rivera.

"Will, what the hell are you doing here?"

"About to give you a much bigger story than what you think you have, Luis," I told him.

And then I filled him in on the whole Bridgeman situation. That I'd been hired to work with Bridgeman on trying to seek out potential victims, after Bridgeman had made a prediction about a Los Angeles official being killed. That I was operating under a no-publicity order, and why. And that Bridgeman had made a similar prediction some four years before, in Helena. And that Ben Franks was going to call him about that. And that Luis should work with the guy, who'd very much like to get out of Helena.

"I'll try, Will," Luis promised me. Then, being the sharp and good reporter that he is, Luis asked me – "Okay, Will – what's in this for you? Why are you doing this?"

And here is where I had to draw the line with Luis.

"Luis, I can't answer your question right now. You have to trust me on this."

There was a pause, while Luis thought about what I had just answered him.

"Come on, Luis," I urged. "You know me."

"Well, okay, Will. Okay for now…"

"That's good enough for me, Luis. Now. One more thing. Please don't use my name in anything you write. Trust me – my name in any of the coverage would be bad. But more important, Luis, keeping my name out of the coverage may lead to an even bigger story, if what I'm suspecting, turns out to be true."

"Man – retirement is bad for you. You're talking in even more riddles than you used to."

Luis paused, then continued.

"Will, did I hear – bigger? And can you put that together with – exclusive?"

"Yes. Bigger. And exclusive. To you – and Ben Franks, working along with you."

After a few seconds, Luis gave me his answer.

"Okay, Will – we got a deal."

"Good. Now, Luis, I am pretty sure that Bridgeman will be showing up at the motel, any minute now. Remember? I told you he wanted publicity about his prediction of a killing here in Los Angeles? So I am 99 per cent sure he'll be here, any minute now, to start pushing for it, with you and the other media."

I gave Luis a description of Bridgeman. And then I told him one more thing.

"Luis, it is important that no one knows that I gave you this tip. So please play it in your story, as if Bridgeman searched you out, when he came here to the scene. He wanted to tell you about his prediction. Until then, you didn't know anything about him or the prediction. You were just here, covering the councilman's killing by his wife. You were not looking for Bridgeman. He came looking for you. No one can know that I gave you this tip."

"But – if when you're talking to Bridgeman, he gives you my name, then that's okay for me to be mentioned in the story."

"Understood, Will. Hey! I see a guy looking like Bridgeman, just walking up to the crime scene tape. I'm gonna make sure my Press Badge/Los Angeles Times is very clear and readable on my jacket. And then, I'll just stroll over in his direction…and snare him into approaching me."

"Go for it, Luis," I said as he clicked off my phone.

Keeping myself out of the line of sight of the motel crime scene room, I watched as Luis wandered into the area where an agitated Ross Bridgeman was leaning against the crime scene tape, looking like he wanted to break the tape and move up to the crime scene.

Luis maneuvered himself into Bridgeman's direct line of sight, angling his body so that his press badge was right in front of Bridgeman.

Bridgeman saw the badge and immediately shifted his attention to Luis. He gestured the reporter over and started talking to him. After a few seconds of back and forth, Luis motioned for Bridgeman to follow him, away from the motel.

Good going, Luis!

CHAPTER TWENTY-SEVEN

A short while later, after the deceased councilman had been shipped to the morgue, his wife taken to jail, and the unfortunate secretary sent home, Dan Foster spoke to the rest of us, assembled in the motel room.

"Effective now, Major Crimes is taking over this case."

"You talking about tonight's shooting?" Captain Klinger asked.

"Yes. That. But also the handling of Ross Bridgeman, henceforth."

"What kind of handling of Bridgeman do you mean?" I asked. "His prediction came through. He's bound to get all the publicity that he wanted. Seems to me that our working with Bridgeman is over, anyway."

And then, on purpose, I added..." Except maybe if Bridgeman has something else in mind."

Foster looked at me, not at all certain what I was talking about.

"Jonas, what the hell does that mean?"

"It means – I think Bridgeman is planning something more. What it is, I don't know. But there is something. And it goes beyond this particular prediction."

Foster waved his finger, side to side, at all of us.

"We don't want Los Angeles to turn into a circus! With the media running around, looking for more people whom Bridgeman can predict will be killed. I'll be making that point very clear to Bridgeman. I'll put him in jail, if I have to –in order to enforce it."

Captain Klinger jumped back into the discussion.

"Jim, I'm inclined to agree with Will. At least to the point, where I want to keep an eye on Bridgeman. Not any kind of close surveillance. But just to keep tabs on him. See if he laps up the publicity on this one, and that's the end of it. Or, if he starts doing something else. I have no idea what that might be. But I'd feel more comfortable about things, if I was aware of his movements. His actions."

I knew better than to add my two cents to what Klinger had

said. He'd made the necessary point to Foster. And since Foster didn't like me – the rent-a-cop—I kept quiet.

Foster nodded at Klinger.

"Okay, you want to waste your manpower like that, go right ahead."

Foster looked around the room. At Klinger. At Charlie. And at me.

"But if anything significant does turns up, you need to let me know. Is that understood? Is that clearly understood?"

CHAPTER TWENTY-EIGHT

The news coverage the next few days was dominated by the murder of Councilman Edward Lyle.

But even more prominent was the news that Ross Bridgeman had predicted Lyle's death, weeks before it happened. And this was topped by the information fed to Luis Rivera by Ben Franks, that Bridgeman had made a similar prediction in Helena, that also had come true.

It was clear to us – Klinger, Charlie and me – that Bridgeman no longer needed the services of the LAPD, or me.

I'd had no word from Bridgeman. No calls. No dropping by my office.

I checked with Charlie. No Bridgeman contacts there, either.

So, I decided, if I wanted to follow up with my suspicions about what Bridgeman might be planning, then I had to get back into his presence.

Which explains why I was standing outside the Best RX store in Reseda, waiting for him to come out. I knew from our previous appointments, what time his shift ended.

The thermometer had climbed to its usual high 90's for late August, and I was uncomfortable, waiting outside for Bridgeman. I was just about to go into the store, when Bridgeman came out.

He wasn't happy to see me.

"What do you want?" was his greeting.

"And a happy hello to you, too, Ross," I said back. "Good to see you. Life's been pretty good the last few days?"

"No thanks to you."

He pointed his finger at me.

"You didn't believe. You did not believe in the power that I have. To predict."

I nodded.

"Well, you got me there," I agreed. "Two out of two. Helena and here. Pretty impressive."

I paused for a few seconds.

"But now I'm wondering – what's next, Ross? Going to move to another town? And another prediction? Think you can go three for three?"

"What I do in the future is none of your concern," Bridgeman snapped back at me.

"Not so sure that's true, Ross. You see, I figure you have something bigger planned. No. Not another prediction. Something more important."

Damn! For whatever the reason, what I said seemed to shake Bridgeman. Startle him a bit.

"You don't know what you're talking about!" he snapped.

I pushed.

"I wouldn't be so sure of that, Ross. "I know something's up. I just need some more time to figure out what it is."

Bridgeman stared at me.

I stared back.

Then he walked away.

I didn't follow. I'd accomplished what I'd set out to do. I'd gotten across to Bridgeman that I sensed he was planning something, and that I was going to try and find out what it was.

Let him chew on that!

CHAPTER TWENTY-NINE

Jonas.
Again, Jonas.
Just as everything is setting up well.
Here comes Jonas. Looking. Looking.
He cannot know what I am planning! He cannot know!
Just some more time, now.
And then everyone will know our wrath.
But in the meantime, if Jonas continues to meddle...
I will have to deal with him.

CHAPTER THIRTY

After seeing Bridgeman, I went back to my office in Woodland Hills, to find the two most important women of my life, Lucy and Rose, huddled over Rose's computer.

"Your wife is not only beautiful," Rose said to me. "She is also Number One with a computer."

"A number one hacker, Rose," Lucy said.

She waved her finger at Rose and me.

"And that's something we need to keep between us."

"Looks like you've found something," I said. "Going to share it?"

"Uh huh," Lucy answered. "I've managed to get into some of the Best RX personnel files. It wasn't easy. They have a pretty good firewall. But I have gotten in."

"And is Ross Bridgeman listed as one of their employees?"

"Yes. Don't think I've gotten all of the entries on his file yet. But I've gotten part of it. And he has an interesting pattern of employment."

"What do you mean?"

"Well, it appears as if Bridgeman likes to move – every two or so years. The files show him going off the payroll in one city, and then being hired anew in another city."

I said, "In other words, he is not an ongoing, continuing employee, but a periodic employee at each place, where he does come onto the payroll."

"Yes."

I thought for a moment. "Okay, that's interesting. But I don't think that fact is important in itself. I'm more interested in knowing what cities he's been living in."

I thought for a moment.

"I managed to drag out of Bridgeman a short list of cities where he said he had lived, before coming to Los Angeles."

I checked the Bridgeman file on my desk.

"The list includes:

Lincoln, Nebraska

Helena, Montana

Santa Fe, New Mexico
Phoenix, Arizona
And Los Angeles, of course."

"Is it possible for you to check those personnel files and see if Bridgeman worked for Best RX in any other cities?"

I thought for a moment.

"Here's why I want to know. Something's driving this guy. I'm betting it goes back to something that happened to him, back several years. So, if we can have that history, it might be helpful."

Lucy considered my request.

"Shouldn't be a problem. Once I can get Bridgeman's full employee file. Remember, I only have managed to get out part of his file."

CHAPTER THIRTY-ONE

For Lucy to get back into the Best RX personnel files turned out to be more difficult than had been anticipated. Lucy explained this to me, the day after she, Rose and I had met in my office.

"I suspect one of their IP people has discovered that someone gained access to their system. So now, they've tightened things up, and I'm sure they are reviewing everything."

"Will you be able to get back in?" I asked.

"At some point, yes."

"How long do you think it will be, before you can do so?" I asked.

"Not sure. Could be days. Could be weeks. Depends on how serious a reprogramming effort they make."

Given this information, I decided it was time for Charlie, Captain Klinger and me to sit down and discuss what we could – and should –be doing with Ross Bridgeman.

"He's not contacting you at all, anymore?" Klinger asked me.

"Nope. Last contact I had, was when I met him outside the Best RX store where he's working. He pretty much told me to get lost. He didn't need me – any of us – anymore."

"Charlie? Have you had any contact with him?"

Charlie shook his head.

"No."

"And as far as we can see, Bridgeman is now an A-number-one model citizen? Doing nothing out of the ordinary?"

"Not even crossing against the light," I said.

Klinger looked at me.

"Will, do you still feel Bridgeman is up to something? That he's planning something for the future?"

"Yes, I do," I answered.

"But no idea what that might be?"

"No idea," Klinger turned to Charlie.

"Charlie? What about you? What do you feel about all of this?"

Charlie shook his head.

"This one's got me, Captain. I don't see anything that says to me, that Bridgeman has anything negative planned for the future."

He shook his head again.

"But if there's one thing I know about my partner Will, when he suspects ...there's usually something to it."

Klinger took up a piece of paper from his desk, studied it, and then spoke to Charlie and me.

"I'm looking at what it's been costing for us to be observing – and that's what we're now doing – observing Ross Bridgeman. Will, the main cost, at present, is what we're paying you."

"Hey, Captain," I interrupted Klinger, "I'll stop taking the consulting fee..."

"Not acceptable," Klinger interrupted me back. "You work for me, you get paid."

"Thank you."

Klinger smiled, then added, "consider it back pay for all of the hard times I gave you, when you were still on the Job."

Klinger went silent again, and then he spoke.

"Okay. I have an idea. It's probably a total waste of time...but you never know. Will, you said you have a list of cities where Bridgeman lived before he came to Los Angeles?"

"I've got a partial list. We're working now, on getting a more complete list."

"How many cities do you have?"

"Four, including Helena."

"And the others are...?" Klinger asked.

"Lincoln, Nebraska

"Santa Fe, New Mexico

"Phoenix, Arizona"

"Do we know when he was in the four cities?" Klinger asked.

"Well, we know it was between the years 1997 and when he arrived here in Los Angeles, in 2002. That's five years. So, if we gave about a year and a half to each city, it would mean:

1997-1998 in Lincoln

1998-1999 in Helena

1999-2000 in Santa Fe

2000-2001 in Phoenix"

"Okay. I'm going to go way out on a limb here," Klinger said. "Except for Helena, I'm going to call the chiefs in those cities and ask them to help us out. I'll tell them we're trying to build a case –

on a confidential basis – about someone who has predicted the deaths of public officials.   And those predictions have come true, in at least two cities – Helena and Los Angeles.   And the question we're trying to get answered is: have there been any killings of public officials in their cities? In the correct years, of course. And if so, can my representatives – that's you two – talk to the responsible homicide detectives?"

"Then you two need to follow up, in each of those cities, to see if we have anything."

"What do you think? We have a feasible plan here? Or am I way too far out, on this one?"

Klinger grinned at me.

"I mean, Will, it sure isn't by the book, now is it? Not my style...but what the hell..."

CHAPTER THIRTY-TWO

"The world is full of surprises."

Did someone once say that?

Is that a famous saying that I'm quoting?

Damned if I know.

But I do know this: if nobody has said it before – "The world is full of surprises" – then I'm going to say it now.

Because the world really *is* full of surprises.

In each of the cities Charlie and I called, we connected with a detective who told us that – yes – there had been a killing involving a high-up government official. Each killing coincided with what we had figured would be the timing for Bridgeman being in that city.

And if that wasn't enough to shake us up – turns out that none of the cases were solved. The homicides were still open on their books.

Did they have any leads on who the killer might be? Did they know anything about the killer?

Here, we drew a blank. No clues. Nothing to tie Bridgeman to the killings – other than the fact that he was living in each city, when each killing occurred.

Of course, for each city, the detectives with whom we spoke got all hot and bothered about the possibilities of catching the killer, and they said they'd send complete files asap – which they did.

Now, four days later, Charlie and I were meeting again with Captain Klinger. I summarized for the captain what we had learned.

"In addition to talking to the detectives who handled the homicide investigations in each city, we've studied the files they sent us. Our conclusions?"

"First, these were thorough, good investigations, even though no arrests were made."

"Second, we think they may all have been committed by the same individual. Plenty of similarities. The victims were alone. The sites were quiet, isolated. The killings were clean, well planned. Everything looked controlled. No rage or other uncontrolled emotion evident."

"Third, no hint that these might have been killings for money. None of the victims had been robbed."

"Fourth, and this one's on the negative side, we didn't find any evidence that would tie Bridgeman to the killings."

"Too bad about that," Klinger said. "No Bridgeman connection at all?"

"None," I replied.

"But Will and I did discuss one thing in our favor," Charlie said. "The timing of these homicides. In all the cases, Bridgeman, according to the Best RX employment records, *was* in each city – when each homicide took place."

"Only problem there, of course," I pointed out, "Is that we are not supposed to have had access to those records."

I'd had to fill in both Klinger and Charlie on what Lucy had done. I'd not identified Lucy, though. Instead, I kept it vague – that I'd found a hacker on my own, and paid him in cash, out of my consulting fee.

"Yeah, but I think we can bluff our way around that problem, when we interview Bridgeman," Charlie said.

"Yes, Captain," I seconded Charlie. "We're feeling pretty good on that point. We just tell Bridgeman that we are aware of these unsolved murders, and they did occur while he was in each of those cities – that's four for four, if we include Helena – and that's way too much to be coincidental...etc...etc..."

"When are you bringing Bridgeman in for questioning?" Klinger asked.

"Tomorrow afternoon," I said. "When he comes off his shift at Best RX."

CHAPTER THIRTY-THREE

The next day, Charlie and I were waiting for Bridgeman as he exited the Best RX store.

When he came out, we flanked him on both sides.

"Hello, Ross," I said. "We'd like to talk with you, please. At the Stationhouse."

"About what?" Bridgeman asked.

"Just some things we want to clear up," Charlie told him. "Won't take long."

Bridgeman stood firmly in place.

"I don't have to talk to you," he challenged.

"No. You don't *have* to talk to us," I told him. "But if you make us go to the trouble of getting a warrant, so that we can question you – well, that's a whole different ballgame."

"Handcuffs and all," Charlie said. "Now, do you really want that? Instead, why not just come along with us now? Won't take long. And then we'll bring you back here, so you can pick up your car. Okay?"

After a few seconds of silence, Bridgeman gave a slight nod and we took him to Charlie's unmarked car, for the short trip to the Stationhouse.

Once there, we brought Bridgeman into one of the interview rooms.

"We'll be back in a few minutes," Charlie told him, after we'd seated him at the table.

And then we left him there for almost an hour. Standard operating procedure. Intended to make the interviewee nervous, uptight, angry – and thus more likely to make mistakes during the interview.

When we did come back, as was our usual good cop-bad cop procedure, Charlie started the questioning.

"Ross, we know you moved around a lot, before coming to Los Angeles. You lived in at least four different cities:
Lincoln, Nebraska
Helena, Montana

Santa Fe, New Mexico

Phoenix, Arizona."

"How come you were moving around so much?"

Bridgeman showed some surprise as Charlie added Lincoln to the three other cities that Bridgeman had previously told me about. But he quickly recovered.

"I like to move. Nothing says I can't do that."

No, of course not," I jumped in. "But there's a curious thing about all those cities. In each one, a government official was murdered. And the cases have never been solved."

Again, a slight bit of surprise by Bridgeman, but he quickly overcame it.

Charlie asked, "Do you remember those cases from when you were in the cities, Ross?"

"No," Bridgeman answered. "I don't remember any of them."

"You didn't make any predictions about the murders? Like you did, here, and in Helena?" I asked.

"No."

"I'm curious about something," I continued. "How come you made your predictions in Helena and in Los Angeles – but not in the other cities?"

"Because I didn't have the kind of information in those cities, like I did in Helena and Los Angeles."

"So, Ross," Charlie picked up the questioning again, "what are your future plans? I mean, are you settling in Los Angeles for the long term? Or are you planning to move somewhere else?"

"None of your business," Bridgeman said.

Clearly, the interview wasn't going anywhere. We knew it. And Bridgeman knew it. I decided a bit of intimidation was about all that I had left to hit him with, so I did.

"We're going to make it our business, if you step out of line! We'll be watching you, Bridgeman. We know you're up to something. And we won't allow it. Not here in Los Angeles."

Bridgeman looked at me and at Charlie. A slight smile caught the edges of his mouth.

"Can you take me back to my car, now?"

CHAPTER THIRTY-FOUR

Charlie arranged for a black and white to take Bridgeman back to Best RX.

Once the officer escorted Bridgeman out of the room, Charlie looked at me, held his hands palms up, and sighed.

"Will, I don't know where we go from here."

"Charlie," I answered, "The damn guy is guilty. His being in all those same cities? With those unsolved murders of public officials? Too many of them to be a coincidence!"

"Okay, I'll give you that. But how do we specifically tie him to the murders? What's his motive? *Why* would he commit those murders?"

We both were silent for a moment, and then an idea started to take form in my head.

"Charlie, can you get your copies of the police reports from Lincoln, Helena, Santa Fe and Phoenix, and bring them in here?"

Charlie left the room and came back a couple of minutes later, carrying the four reports.

I took two of them, and left two for Charlie.

"Take a look at each report, and regarding the official who was killed, is there any information about what his job was? Or his title? I'll check these two, you check those."

It took us just a couple of minutes to find the information. There was a blackboard in the room and I went to it.

"Okay, tell me what you got for Lincoln."

"Deputy Director of Budgets, State Highway Commission"

"And for Phoenix?"

"Supervisor, Buildings Inspection Department."

"Now, for my two, I've got – for Helena – Department of Sanitation. And for Santa Fe, the victim was the Director of Traffic and Safety."

I looked at all four descriptions and then at Charlie.

"Okay," I challenged him, "tell me what you see all four victims having in common."

Charlie shrugged.

"Something we already knew. They're all high level city or

state officials. Maybe elected. Maybe appointed. Maybe career."

"But," I pointed out to him, "They all also had something else in common. They ran departments that provided services to the public.

"So ask yourself this, Charlie. Why would anyone want to knock off people like these? My answer? Because they're pissed at them. And why do people get pissed at bureaucrats like these? Because, these bureaucrats have screwed up. Done something wrong.

"On this point, I remember my first interview with Bridgeman. I was asking him about the guy who was killed in Helena. The victim was the head of the Department of Sanitation. And when I questioned Bridgeman about him, the first thing he said was that the man had just been convicted of taking bribes from wealthy homeowners to get preferential treatment for snow removal."

"You know me, Charlie." I couldn't help making a joke about that. And I said, "So the guy made money out of snow. Imaginative – even if illegal."

"What did Bridgeman then do?"

"He banged his fist down on the table and shouted at me...'He did wrong! Can't you see the justice in what happened to him?'"

Charlie thought about what I had said.

"But Will, so Bridgeman had a hard on for that particular person. How does this tie in to all the other killings?"

"Because here's what I think, Charlie. I think something happened to Bridgeman. Something bad. And it involved a public official or some governing body screwing him."

"And so he set out for revenge. The result: the murders in those cities. All tied to time periods when Bridgeman was in each of those cities."

Charlie didn't say anything.

I went on. "Figure it this way, Charlie. All four murdered public officials were involved with bureaus or departments whose actions directly affect people like you, me, Bridgeman.

Highways
Building Inspection
Sanitation
Traffic and Safety."

Charlie started nodding in agreement.

71

"Yes. It *is* beginning to make sense now. I can see it."

Charlie thought for a minute.

"But you know what, Will? What's still missing is what specific beef does Bridgeman have with the bureaucratic world? What did that world do to *him,* that could get him so angry, as to start killing people, like we're thinking he's done? Or, to put it simply – *what was his particular motive"?*

"I don't have the answer," I said. "But I'm going back to my office, to hopefully find it. I want to call Ben Franks. Maybe he has some history on Bridgeman in his files, stuff that we don't already know about."

"And I've got another idea I want Rose and Lucy to work on. A way of getting more information about Bridgeman – maybe."

CHAPTER THIRTY-FIVE

On the way back to my office in Woodland Hills, from the Stationhouse in Chatsworth, I noticed that the rush hour traffic was a bit lighter than usual. It figures, I said to myself. People have already taken off for the Labor Day Holiday weekend that starts the day after tomorrow, on Friday.

When I reached the office, the first thing I did was place a call to Ben Franks in Helena. Like last time, I caught him at the Independent Record.

"Hey, Will," Ben said when I identified myself, "I've been meaning to call and thank you. It looks like I might be getting an offer, to come to the Times. Rivera and his editor liked my work on Bridgeman."

"That's great, Ben. Hope it happens."

"What can I do for you, Will?"

"This is all off the record, Ben. It may lead to something good in the future, but right now, off the record. Understood?"

"Understood."

"Okay. It's about Bridgeman. Looking over my notes, I don't think I ever learned what place he lived in – before he started moving around. Did he ever tell you, where he started? He told me he was a widower. I'm wondering where he might have lived, when his wife was still alive."

"Can you hold on a minute, Will?" Ben asked. "Let me check my notes."

"Okay. I'll hold."

And I did, for a minute or two, until Ben came back on the line.

"Will? What I have here, is that Bridgeman's original hometown was Knoxville, Tennessee. That was in 1973."

"Do your notes tell you anything about his family?"

"No. Just that it was his hometown, and that he was living there in 1973."

"Ben, this helps. Thanks."

"Rose!" I shouted out to the reception room of the office.

Rose came marching in.

"Nu?" she asked.

This was Rose's standard reply, whenever I called for her.

For those of you not familiar with the Yiddish language, – "nu" – as Rose had informed me, is one of those very useful words that has lots of meanings. In this case, it was Rose's shorthand way of asking, "What is it you want?"

"I need you to get on your computer, and do two things. First, see if you can find any trace of Ross Bridgeman living in Knoxville, Tennessee. This would be about 1973."

"And second, if you do find him living there, see if you can find any Knoxville newspaper story that reports on the killing of a high level public official. Maybe city, or county or state. This would also be in 1973, or maybe 1974."

"And Rose, I need this stuff, yesterday."

"Understood," Rose said, as she turned and hurried from the office.

The private line on my office phone rang, and when I picked up, it was Lucy, calling from her office.

"You still there?" I asked. "Thought you'd be heading home. What with the holiday weekend coming up."

"I was intending to," Lucy answered. "But I thought I'd take a crack at Best RX, to see if I could get back into their personnel files. And I did!"

"Great! Does that include the rest of Bridgeman's file?"

"Yes, it does."

"So can you please print out a complete list of the cities where he's worked for Best RX – and in what years? And email or fax me that list? Before you go home?"

"You are a slave driver!"

"But one that you love."

"That, too."

I turned serious.

"As soon as possible, Lucy. I really need it."

For the next 45 minutes, I took out and drank two diet cream sodas from our small office refrigerator. I straightened out the papers on my desk. I went to the bathroom, even though I didn't have to. This is how I spent the time, waiting impatiently, to see what Rose and Lu could turn up for me.

Hey, was I a victim of the Technology Age? I guess I was. But looked at from the other end of the tunnel, I was someone waiting to benefit from that Age. All it would take, are good reports from Rose and from Lucy.

Rose was first to come in with the results of her research.

"Thanks to taxes he was paying on a house he owned, I was able to find that Ross Bridgeman was living in Knoxville, Tennessee in 1973."

"Good. And did you look for any newspaper stories about a high-level public official being killed around that time in the Knoxville area?"

"I looked. No story like that, Will."

Rose held up a computer printout sheet.

"But I think I found something very important. Look at this," she said, handing over the sheet.

It was a reproduction of a story from the Knoxville News Sentinel.

June 12, 1973 ... Knoxville

A mother and her three children were killed this morning, when their car was blindsided by a pickup truck at the intersection of Willis Avenue and 14th Street. The mother, Clare Bridgeman, 37, was driving her children to school. The youngsters have been identified as 11-year-old George, 8 year old Chester and 4 year old Christopher.

They are survived by the husband, Ross Bridgeman, 42, who was not in the car. At the time of the accident, Mr. Bridgeman was on his way, in a separate vehicle, to his place of employment, Real Teck Hardware, where he was assistant manager.

The driver of the pickup, Stacey Callister, was uninjured.

According to Police Chief Richard Klasky, "An ongoing problem at that intersection has led to this tragic event. It is well known that improved approach roads, better sight lines and a traffic light all are needed—and in fact – had been ordered several months ago. Why those improvements were not yet made is beyond me."

The News Sentinel, investigating Chief Klasky's comments has learned that the original funding for the improvements, budgeted *at $250,000, was diverted by the State Highway Commission, to pay for roadwork needed, prior to the recent opening of the Tennessee Annual Faire.*

"Motive! We got motive," I shouted, as I looked at the News Sentinel story.

I explained to Rose. "Charlie and I have been trying to figure out *why* someone like Bridgeman seems so intent on killing public officials. And this story gives us a feasible reason. It shows that a bureaucratic decision cost him his family! And as far as I'm concerned, it gives him a motive for revenge."

"And I suspect – once we start checking the cities where Bridgeman lived over the years – based on his employment by Best RX, we're going to find that Bridgeman looks for a new dose of revenge every few years, by killing another public official."

I needed to bring Charlie up to date on this latest development, but first, I needed to check out if my revenge theory made any sense. I thought it did. But I needed something more concrete.

I called Lucy at her office.

"Have you finished pulling Bridgeman's personnel file from Best RX?"

"Just done."

"When did he first start working for Best RX? And where?"

"Hold on," Lucy said.

Then, "He started with them in February, 1974. In Nashville, Tennessee.

"Good. Okay, please send me the complete file."

"Will do."

I hung up and called Rose in again.

"Back onto your computer again, please," I told her. "Look at the daily newspapers in Nashville, Tennessee, beginning in February, 1974. See if you can find any stories about a public official being murdered. And again, Rose – please – as fast as you can."

This was a simple one for Rose to research, and a few minutes later, she was back in my office.

"I found this one," she said, handing me the computer printout of a story in the Nashville Tennessean:

Nashville, Tenn…June 10, 1974

The body of Nashville Metropolitan Council member Merton Ogilvy was discovered late last night in Ogilvy's car, parked in the driveway of his home.

According to Nashville police, Ogilvy had been shot multiple times and was dead at the scene.

Councilman Ogilvy recently was acquitted of two counts of bribery, following a trial in which he was accused of accepting $40,000.00 in illegal campaign contributions. At the time, Ogilvy was serving on a special Council committee considering changes in the city's building code which some have charged were unduly favorable to real estate developers in the county.

In response to reporters' questioning, Police said they are following up on several leads, but could provide no details.

It fit! I decided my revenge theory definitely fit

I figured this probably was the first of Bridgeman's revenge killings, after his family had been wiped out in that car accident that the police claimed could have been avoided, if certain road, signage and traffic light improvements had been made. But they hadn't been made, because the funds were diverted to other uses. And Bridgeman no longer had his family.

And so a revenge killer was the result.

I was ready to bet, that when Lucy sent me that list of cities that Bridgeman worked in, for Best RX, we'd find some more newspaper reports of the killing of government officials in those cities.

I called Rose in for a third time.

"It's late. You need to go home. But can you come in early tomorrow? I want you to take the list Lucy is sending, of Bridgeman's employment record with Best RX. Look at that list. See the cities where he worked for the company. Then, check out the daily newspapers in those cities, to see if there were any unsolved homicides of public officials – and this is the important part – while Bridgeman was living on that city. That's the list that I want. Cities where Bridgeman lived, with newspaper stories reporting on the killing of any public officials."

"I'll be in at eight in the morning," Rose promised.

After Rose left, I called Charlie. He was at home.

"Charlie," I said, "we're going to need an early morning meeting with Klinger. I've got new information here, that I think makes it look like Ross Bridgeman is a serial killer — motivated by revenge!"

CHAPTER THIRTY-SIX

"How many murders do you think you've been able to link Bridgeman to?" Captain Klinger asked me to repeat the number, the shock evident on his face.

It was shortly after 9 on Thursday, the next morning, and Klinger, Charlie and I were meeting in Klinger's office in the Stationhouse on Devonshire in Chatsworth.

"Eight," I answered. "So far, we've found eight, unsolved homicides of public officials, in cities where Bridgeman was living, *at the time of the killings.* None of the homicides has been solved."

"And we're not through looking. Rose is in the office right now, tracking Bridgeman's employment record with Best RX. Every city where he shows on their payroll – she's doing the research to see if there's an unsolved homicide of a public official."

"We think, too," Charlie added, "that Bridgeman may try to kill another official here in Los Angeles. Despite his claims to the media – about having predicted Councilman Lyle's death – he knows this one was a fluke. We think that he might have someone else in mind."

I said, "We've spoken to the detectives in charge of each of the killings in the different cities, and they want to know when they can come out here, and have a crack at breaking whatever alibis Bridgeman tries on them."

And then I added, "We need to pick Bridgeman up again, Captain. We need to do it today. We need to question him about these eight cities and the homicides in each."

"First, we need to see Dan Foster," Klinger said.

Seeing the look on my face, Klinger anticipated my objection.

"Will, you've done a great job on this." He grimaced. "But you know Foster. He made it clear to us that he was taking over the investigation. So, we need to go to him, with this information."

"Yeah, I know you're right," I agreed. "But I don't think I should be at that meeting. You know his feelings about rent-a-cops."

"I don't care about his feelings!" Klinger said. "You've done the work. So you're the one to present your findings to Foster."

Klinger flipped on his intercom.

"Evelyn, please get me Dan Foster at Major Crimes downtown. Tell him it's urgent that I talk to him – now."

CHAPTER THIRTY-SEVEN

"How sure are you about all this?" Dan Foster asked, after Will had reviewed, for him, his findings about the eight homicides in the eight cities.

"We can verify that Bridgeman was living in each city, when each homicide occurred. We have newspaper clippings reporting on the homicides during those same time periods. And we've spoken to the detectives in charge of each investigation in each city. None of the homicides has been solved."

"It looks solid to us, Dan," Klinger said. "We need to bring Bridgeman in, and start to sweat him on this."

Foster glanced at his wristwatch and grimaced.

"I'm leaving town in an hour. Gone up to my cabin in Idaho. Not back until Sunday night."

"No problem," Klinger said. "We certainly can start the process with Bridgeman. Bring him in. See what we can develop."

Clearly, Foster had a dilemma. He wanted to keep control of the investigation. At the same time, he had his plans for the Labor Day weekend.

"Okay," he allowed. "Bring him in. See what you can do."

Foster jabbed his finger toward Klinger, Charley and me.

"But let's be clear about this. Once I'm back, no arm wrestle over who handles the investigation. Major Crimes. Understood?"

He waited until all three of us nodded our understanding.

"Okay, get to it," Foster said. "Now, I got a bunch else to work on before I leave..."

CHAPTER THIRTY-EIGHT

By about 12:30, Klinger, Charlie and I were back in the Northridge LAPD stationhouse.

We dropped Klinger off, and then Charlie and I went directly to the Best RX drugstore in Reseda, on Tampa at Sherman Way, to bring Bridgeman in for questioning.

Only problem – Bridgeman wasn't at the store.

"He didn't show up for his shift today," the store manager told us.

"What time was he supposed to be here?" I asked.

"He was due in, at 11 AM, with his shift running until 6 PM."

The manager shook his head.

"First time this has ever happened, with him. He's usually very reliable and on time."

"Did you call him?"

"Tried. But the phone's been disconnected."

We had Bridgeman's home address with us –he had an apartment on Variel Street in Chatsworth -- so we got back into the car and 15 minutes later, we arrived at the two story building containing Bridgeman's unit.

We found the apartment. It was on the second floor, in the rear.

Charlie rang the bell, and we waited.

Nothing.

Charlie rang again – this tine holding down the button for several seconds.

Still nothing.

We returned to the first floor and hunted down the manager in apartment #1.

"Bridgeman? He's gone. Left yesterday. Didn't want to leave a forwarding address. You know. For any mail. But that didn't seem to matter to him."

"Any idea where he went?" I asked. "Did he mention anything? Any place?"

"Not to me, he didn't. But that's not surprising. He was one definite loner, that guy. Never wanted to talk. Just about got a 'hello' out of him, whenever I saw him. And even then, not every time."

CHAPTER THIRTY-NINE

Back at the Stationhouse, Charlie – with Klinger smoothing the way – worked on getting an all-points bulletin out on Bridgeman. It went out fast. By 4 PM. Much faster than usual, thanks to Klinger doing some heavy pushing at the administrative end. No easy job on this, the tail-end of a shortened work week, due to the upcoming Labor Day holiday weekend.

"Well," Charlie said to Will, "I don't know what the hell else we can do now. Have to wait and hope the all-points turns up something for us."

I shook my head.

"Don't much think that's going to happen," I said.

"Wonder where he's headed, and why," Charlie said. "Didn't think we scared him enough, at our meeting with him – so he'd take off so suddenly."

"I'm thinking, Charlie, that we didn't scare him at all. I have a feeling that what Bridgeman is doing now, is moving ahead on his plan."

"In other words," Charlie picked up on my thoughts, "you think he's making his Los Angeles move? That he's got some official in his sights for killing? And that he's now starting that process?"

"Makes sense to me," I said. "For one thing, this is the first time he's screwed up his job with Best RX. All the previous times he's left, he must have kept it friendly and clean – so he'd be hired in whatever next city he showed up, if there was a Best RX store there."

"Not this time, though. He just didn't show up. Didn't call. Obviously, he doesn't care about any bad impression he was leaving with the store manager."

Both Charlie and I were quiet for a short while.

Then Charlie got up and started pacing around.

"I wonder what the hell he's up to," he said.

"I think we may be close to finding out," I answered.

CHAPTER FORTY

Nothing for me to do at the Stationhouse. And I'd told Rose to go home. So I gave myself the same advice.

When I got there, Lucy greeted me with a kiss on her lips and a tall glass of water in her hand.

I enjoyed the kiss and took a long draw on the water. Both helped to ease my tensions.

"No sign of Bridgeman, yet?" Lucy asked.

"No sign," I confirmed.

"Listen," I said, "the work that you did – getting that Best RX personnel information – that was really good. It's been critical to helping us understand what Bridgeman is doing."

"Glad I could help. Did any more cities come up, with possible homicides, while Bridgeman was living there?"

"One more. So including Los Angeles, we've got a total of nine cities."

I shook my head.

"But just one concerns me right now. Los Angeles."

"You don't think he's just taken off? Left the area? Worried about you picking him up?"

"No. I think Bridgeman sees Los Angeles as the 'end of the game' location. Whatever it is that's driving him, I think he feels it's here, that his final move needs to be made."

Lucy took my hand and led me toward the dining room. A wise woman – trying to get my mind off of the case for a while.

And she succeeded.

As I've told you before, about a year ago, Lucy, whose cooking ability had pretty much been limited to eggs, decided it was time that we ate more at home, and less in restaurants.

And just like she is about anything she decides to do. Lucy set a high goal for her cooking capabilities. She intended to become – to use her phrase – "a chef-level cook." About a dozen books and many kitchen hours later, Lucy had now achieved her goal.

So tonight, while most husbands had to be satisfied with a steak, or possibly hamburgers, or even spaghetti and meatballs, Yours Truly dined on – are you ready for this – spring duckling with apricots.

And Lucy let me know that she did not include in the recipe a quarter of a cup of white wine, since that would have nixed the meal for me.

That great dinner was Lucy's way of trying to get my mind away from Bridgeman for a while.

And it worked.

As did the special dessert Lucy then offered me, but which I will not describe here. You'll have to use your imagination.

CHAPTER FORTY-ONE

Everything was fine for the rest of the evening -- until about 4 AM, when I woke up, my mind filled with thoughts of Bridgeman.

Where the hell was he?

What was he planning?

Or was I dead wrong, in thinking he was planning anything?

And that's the way I spent the next three hours – until 7 AM, when I decided to get up and start moving. I don't know what I intended to do – but staying in bed, worrying, wasn't the right ticket.

By 8:30, I was in Denny's – on Burbank just west of Topanga, in Woodland Hills – a coffee shop near my office – and just the opposite of gourmet. Here is where you loaded up on the calories and the vein clogging stuff.

I gave the waitress my order for scrambled eggs, with a side of pancakes, and then I picked up the copy of the Los Angeles Times that I'd bought at the stand just outside the restaurant.

I skimmed the front page and was about to turn to the separate sports section, when one of the headlines, at the top of page 1, hit me. It said:

LOS ANGELES COUNTY FAIR OPENS TODAY FOR 80th Year

State and County Dignitaries Will Attend Opening Ceremony

I stared at the headlines as my brain started churning up some facts.

If I remembered correctly, yesterday, Rose had found a 1973 story in the Knoxville News Sentinel. It reported that Ross Bridgeman's entire family – his wife and his three young sons – had been killed in a car accident at an intersection.

And the key wording that I remembered from that story, was what the chief of police had said. About how the accident should not have happened. Except that some road and intersection construction improvements had been put off – and why.

My close-to-photographic memory played Chief Klasky's words back to me:

"Original funding for the improvements, budgeted at $250,000, was diverted by the State Highway Commission, to pay for roadwork needed prior to the recent opening of the Tennessee State Faire."

So here it was! I'd bet everything I owned on it.

Bridgeman's family had died because of funds diverted for the Tennessee State Faire.

So now, for his revenge, Bridgeman was going after the Los Angeles County Fair!

I read further into the Time's story and learned that an opening ceremony – a ribbon cutting -- was scheduled for 11 AM – today. The ribbon was to be cut by the California Lieutenant Governor. Also taking part in the ceremonies was the chairman of the Los Angeles County Board of Supervisors, top officials of the Fair administration, and several mayors representing Pomona and the many other local communities surrounding the region where the Fair was located.

And the Times story had another interesting point.

A real kicker!

Maybe even the biggest reason of all, to explain why Bridgeman was targeting the Fair.

Last year – 2001—the Fair closed for the first time in its history since World War II. Last year, was when, on September 11th, terrorists had flown their hijacked airplanes into the twin towers in New York.

So, since the Fair was closed last year because of Nine Eleven, this year's opening would be very much in the news. And this would fit right in with Bridgeman's desire for publicity, as he sought his revenge for the deaths of his wife and children.

Hell! If he does something at this Fair, there will be more than enough publicity. That was for sure.

I saw the waitress heading toward me with my order. I got up and put a ten-dollar bill on the table.

"Got to go," I said. "Hope the ten covers everything." And I raced out to my car. I needed to call Charlie! Pronto!

CHAPTER FORTY-TWO

One of the benefits of Klinger having brought me on as a paid consultant, was that I was issued a set of lights that I could put on my roof, if I needed to get from one place to another, in fast time. I used the lights, and the siren I'd also been issued, to make it over to the Northridge Station in about 15 minutes. Of course, it helped that I was going against rush hour traffic.

When I reached the Station, neither Charlie nor Klinger were in yet. Nothing I could do about it. I looked at my watch.

9:05 AM.

One hour and 55 minutes until the ribbon cutting ceremony.

Getting out to Pomona from here, even with the lights and the siren, was at least an hour trip – and most likely, longer than that.

What to do! What to do!

I couldn't do a damn thing. Not on the Job. Just a consultant. Or as Foster would have put it—a rent-a-cop.

Fuck you, Foster. I hope you had four flat tires on your trip out of town for the weekend!

Klinger and Charlie arrived at the same time.

I filled both of them in, on what I was thinking.

"I think you're right, Will," Klinger said. "Now the question is, what can we do about it?"

Klinger drummed his fingers on his desk.

"Okay, here's what we do.

"First, you two have to head out to the Fair. If you leave now, you ought to be there by about 10:30. Not much time to look for Bridgeman, but that's it."

"In the meantime, I'm going to get on the phone to the California State Police, to the Chief of the Pomona Police Department, to the Fairplex management office, and to anyone else I think can help."

Klinger shook his head.

"Trouble is, I'm going to have a hard sell. Look I believe you, Will. But these people I'm calling – well, they've not been involved. At all. If he were here, Dan Foster probably could pull some weight. But he's not."

I interrupted Klinger.

"And there's another problem, I just realized."

"What's that?" Klinger asked.

I told him.

"The only people who even know what Bridgeman looks like – are the three of us! Even if you can get some state troopers out there, plus the local cops, they don't know what Bridgeman looks like. How the hell can they track him? He's sure not going to be looking conspicuous. He won't stand out. So, how will they even recognize him?"

"Only one thing we can do, Captain," Charlie said.

"What's that?"

"We've all got to get the hell out there, then split up, and hope one of us finds him."

CHAPTER FORTY-THREE

For the next few minutes, Charlie, Klinger and I got ready to leave.

Klinger grabbed his phone, with all of his contact numbers in it.

We signed out Glock 45 weapons from the armory.

And we put on bulletproof Kevlar body armor.

We piled into Charlie's car at 9:40, and headed for Pomona, via the 134 East and then, the 210 East.

A total of 56 miles, which the GT claimed was a trip of 1 hour and 5 minutes. Well, we were about to find out.

Once we were underway, Klinger took out his phone and started making his calls.

The first one was to Foster's office, on the off-chance that Foster had not left town. But he had. So Klinger talked to Foster's deputy, who said he'd call someone in Homeland Security, but he wasn't very optimistic about that department being able to move fast enough to be of any help in the next few hours.

Next, Klinger spoke to his Chief, who said he'd call his counterpart at the California Highway Patrol, to see if the latter could arrange for one of their cruisers to meet up with us, and speed our trip to Pomona.

Then Klinger got through to the Pomona Police Department, but as expected, the chief of the department had already left for the Fair grounds. Klinger asked to be patched through to the chief, and Charlie and I listened in on Klinger's side of the conversation.

After identifying himself, Klinger went on to tell the Chief the following.

"Based on investigating work we've done here, we believe there is a lone gunman coming to the Fair this morning, intent on killing the dignitaries at the ribbon cutting ceremony."

Pause for a reply, then Klinger started talking again.

"It's a complicated investigation, Chief. And we can't be absolutely sure we are right, but we're pretty positive we are."

Pause for a reply, then Klinger again talks.

"What we'd like you to do, is contact whatever security

personnel are responsible for the dignitaries involved in the ribbon cutting ceremony, and have that event cancelled."

Pause for a reply, then Klinger again.

"Yes, I can certainly understand your point, Chief. But suppose we *are* right? And the gunman *does* show up and starts shooting? Wouldn't it be better to take this as a serious threat?"

Another pause.

"Okay, Chief. I do appreciate your offer to at least alert the security person in charge of the ribbon cutting, and to bring our information to his attention. Thank you."

Klinger cut the connection and shook his head.

"He doesn't feel confident about what I'm telling him. And I can't blame him. We're coming at him, less than two hours before the event. With no hard facts. Just a theory and our suspicions."

I heard a siren, and looking behind us, I saw a California Highway Patrol car coming up fast on the far left lane.

"Well, at least someone believes us," I said, as Charlie swung in behind the cruiser and we definitely bettered our chances of making it to the Fair in less than 1 hour and 5 minutes.

CHAPTER FORTY-FOUR

By the time we arrived at the Fair, Klinger had made another call, to try and find out exactly where the ribbon cutting was going to take place. The Fair was on a sprawling site, with several entry gates. He learned that the ceremony would take place just outside Gate 17, also known as the Yellow Gate.

Via his contact at CHP—the California Highway Patrol – Klinger was able to get word to the cruiser we were following, so when we reached the area, the cruiser brought us to that area.

It was now 10:35 – twenty-five minutes until the ribbon cutting ceremony.

We came out of our car and looked toward the gate, which was a good quarter of a mile from where we were standing. Between us and the gate, I estimated there were there several thousand Fair visitors, everyone intent on pushing forward, not so much, I guessed, as to witness the ribbon cutting itself, but to then move to Gate 17 and into the Fair grounds.

Looking at what faced us, I turned to Klinger and Charlie.

"Captain? Charlie? I think the best thing for us to do, is to split up. One of us starts at the far left. A second at the far right. And the third person in the center."

Klinger picked up on my thinking.

"Then we all move forward."

Charlie said, "And the objective is to keep the ribbon cutting ceremony at the center of our advance, so we all three end up in that vicinity."

"Unless, of course," I said, "one of us meets up with Bridgeman earlier."

I looked out over the crowd.

"Whoever meets up with Bridgeman, then my thinking is that we need to try and get in real close to him, and disarm him. In a crowd like this, if we start a shooting war with him, especially from any distance, then there will be a lot of civilian casualties."

"Agreed," Klinger said.

"Right," Charlie added

Charlie started off to my left. Klinger to my right. And I

started down the center.

The crowd was a happy one. Mainly families with young children. Occasional older folks. Even some wheelchairs and walkers.

I looked at my watch. It was 10:45. I looked toward where the ribbon cutting ceremony was going to be held. Up on a small elevated stage. Decorated with bunting and ribbons in red, white and blue, along with the American and California flags, and the LA County Fair signage.

I started pushing my way forward – not too hard – didn't want to get anybody mad – get in any kind of an argument. In case Bridgeman was nearby, I didn't want to draw his attention. Alerting him to my being here. He'd surely know why.

Looked for any tall men. When I'd met Bridgeman for the first time, I'd seen that he was almost as tall as me.

Ran into a large party straight ahead. And I do mean large. Must have been a couple of families. Totaling 15-20 people. Took some maneuvering to get around them.

Looked for Charlie on my left and Klinger on my right. Caught occasional glimpses of each of them. They were progressing at about the same pace as I was.

Wondered what Bridgeman's plan was? How would he do whatever it was he was planning? A bomb thrown? Or wrapped in suicide form around his middle, intending to climb up on the platform and to detonate himself?

Or a weapon? Pistol. Good for a few shots, maybe. Or an automatic or semi-automatic...to assault a larger group?

And suppose I was wrong? Suppose he doesn't show up at all? Suppose, instead, he had decided to skip town and was now somewhere else, entirely?

I kept working forward. Stopped a few times when I thought I saw the head of a man who stood taller than the people around him. Not Bridgeman.

By now, I was within 100 to 150 feet of the stage. I looked at it. Saw the Lieutenant Governor in the middle of the dignitaries. Didn't recognize any of the others, but judging by their ready-for-television dark suits and red, solid ties, I figured these were the people who belonged up there as part of the ribbon cutting.

Took another look 360 degrees around me. Had to move a

few steps to my side, because of a cartoon costume figure in the crowd – Pineapple Pete. His mask and attached cap ran taller than me, and blocked my view of the crowd behind him. Pete had a "Free Samples" sign on both the front and back of his costume, and people were grabbing samples enthusiastically.

Still no sign of Bridgeman.

It was almost 11. The dignitaries were now lining up behind a microphone and lectern that were placed at center stage. The Lieutenant Governor was moving toward it. Someone was already at the lectern – looking at some notes. And I figured he was the person who would be introducing the Lieutenant Governor.

I looked to both my left and right. Spotted Charlie and Klinger. Both gave me negative head shakes. They'd not seen Bridgeman, either.

I heard the person at the microphone clearing his voice.

Took one more look around. Annoyed, now, because I had to move again, to see around that Pineapple Pete guy.

Only this time, I realized, the hat and mask were off!

And the rest of the costume was coming off!

And I could see an automatic rifle that the costume had hidden. A rifle that Ross Bridgeman was now swinging toward the stage, taking aim at the Lieutenant Governor.

I took out my weapon and aimed it at Bridgeman.

I hesitated. Too many people between Bridgeman and me. If I fired now, I took the risk of hitting some bystanders.

But what the hell should I do?

I yelled, "GUN!"

And then I yelled: BRIDGEMAN

At the word, GUN, people around me started to scream and to scatter, especially when they saw my weapon.

When I yelled his name, Bridgeman turned in my direction.

He swung his rifle away from the lectern and aimed it at me.

I aimed my weapon back at him…still worried that if I fired, I'd hit some innocent person.

Then Bridgeman changed his mind. He was after bigger game than me. He swung his rifle back toward the Lieutenant Governor. Evidently, no one on the lectern had heard my shouts.

I saw Bridgeman concentrate on aiming.

He left me with a poor choice.

But I had to take it.

I steadied my aim and squeezed off a round.

And damn! I hit him!

Bridgeman started to stumble. But then he steadied. He swung his rifle toward me and fired.

I went to the ground.

I thought I was diving to get out of the line of fire.

But it somehow felt different.

No jolt as I hit the ground.

Instead, everything was soft.

Increasingly dark.

And then it was black.

CHAPTER FORTY-FIVE

"Will. Dear Will. How do you feel?"

I opened my eyes, to see Lucy and Charlie looking down at me. I was in a hospital bed.

"What happened? Where am I?"

"Bridgeman shot you," Charlie said. "Fortunately, the bullet hit the body armor you were wearing. Right near your heart. So you're going to feel sore there for a few days."

"But when you fell from the bullet's impact," Lucy said, "You hit your head on the concrete which is poured in that area. And you were knocked out. You're in the emergency room at the hospital near the Fair."

"What happened to Bridgeman?" I asked.

"Bridgeman is dead," Charlie said. "Your shot brought him down. Then he got up again. And he aimed his weapon at the stage. But he was too weak to steady it, or to fire it."

Charlie thought for a few seconds, and then continued.

"The thing is, when he saw he wasn't going to get a shot at the stage, all the air went out of him. He turned toward me. But he didn't shoot. He just waited. I wasn't going to fire. I figured to take him, alive."

"But when I didn't fire, Bridgeman raised his rifle and pointed it at me. So I had to shoot him. It...it was like...he wanted to die at that point."

EPILOG

It was Tuesday afternoon, following the Labor Day holiday weekend, and Luis Rivera, the crime reporter for the Los Angeles Times, sat across from Captain Klinger, Charlie Black and me. We were in the conference room in the Northridge Stationhouse.

Rivera said, "We received this letter at the Times, via courier, over the weekend. It's from Ross Bridgeman, and it was addressed to me."

Rivera gave each of us a copy, and I read mine.

"Luis, by the time you receive this letter – I'm sending it Friday morning -- you will know the answer to the question you have been asking me – what are my plans for the future?"

"My plans are to kill as many government officials as I can, at today's opening ceremony for the Los Angeles County Fair."

"Why? Because it is Justice."

"Twenty-nine years ago, government officials connected with the Tennessee State Faire, took away money already budgeted for improvements needed to the road where my wife and three sons were later killed, and instead used the money for road improvements for the Faire."

"My family died so the roads to the Faire could be improved!"

"Irresponsible government officials killed my family!"

"And I have made it my Life's work to seek out such negligent and wrongful officials, wherever I can find them. And to kill them."

"Let the bureaucrats, the elected officials, the civil servants know that their irresponsible actions – will not go unnoticed. Nor unpunished!"

"Luis, many times, when we met, you asked me why I predicted publicly the deaths of the government officials in Helena and in Los Angeles."

"Did I really know they were going to die?" You kept asking me.

"And while I told you that, yes, I could predict, and I did know – that was not true. I don't have any special powers like that."

"So, why did I predict? Because, I wanted to make sure, by the time of the Los Angeles Fair, that what I did at the Fair, would get national attention, based on my successful predictions in Helena and Los Angeles."

"And just to answer the questions I know you're asking – in Helena, I did kill that official. They just could never prove it."

"And in Los Angeles, I was really lucky, when that councilman's wife shot him. Otherwise I would have had to kill someone here. Not to worry. I had a list of plenty of deserving candidates."

"And it all worked just right, didn't it, Luis? Thanks to your stories and the other media, everyone will understand *what I did and why* over these many years."

"I can only hope that, as others learn what I have done, they will pick up, where I am ending."

"They will seek out corrupt and negligent public officials – and kill them!"

Roswell Clarence Bridgeman

I broke the silence that followed our reading of Bridgeman's letter.

"His Manifesto," I said. "That's what this is. Bridgeman's Manifesto. Justifying what he did. Sick. Sick. Sick."

"He was insane," Klinger said.

"Yes, nuts," Charlie agreed. "But dangerous as hell."

"You're not going to print this, are you?" I asked Rivera.

"No, the Times is not going to print it," Luis replied. "Sure, it would be a great follow-on story to what happened last Friday."

"But his call for others to pick up where he was ending? Dangerous stuff."

"We don't want his words to encourage anyone."

"He did enough damage, all by himself."

###

YOU REMEMBER...
YOU DIE

SAUL WARSHAW

CONTENTS

CHAPTER 1

THE YEAR...2003

What is it about grandchildren and their suspicions that a grandparent may have committed a murder? Or, been a murder victim?

I ask, because here we are, in the year 2003, and one Allison Morris is seated on the other side of my desk, in my office, in Woodland Hills, California, having just said to me...

"I think my grandfather was murdered. Can you please help me prove it?"

Very similar to a case I had back in 1998, when a couple of grandchildren came in, with their grandmother's diary, in which that deceased lady had written that she had killed her husband. Turns out she didn't, and I did nail the killer...but that's another story for another time.

To set today's scene, I'm Will Jonas, a retired Los Angeles Police Department homicide detective, and for the last eight years, I've been running my own private investigations agency. Sounds impressive, huh? Well, don't get too excited. My "agency" consists of me and my secretary-receptionist-book keeper-Jewish mother-everything helper, Rose Shapiro.

More about Rose and me later, but now, back to topic number one – Allison Morris and her claim that her grandfather had been murdered.

Ms. Morris looked to be in her early twenties. Attractive. Long, brown hair, large brown eyes straddling a straight, not too long, not too short nose, and a mouth in sync with the rest of her face.

It was a refreshing, open face, the kind you don't see much of nowadays, except on those young people lucky enough not to have been beaten up yet, by that thing called Life Experience.

At the moment, Allison's face reflected two things: that she believed what she had just told me about her grandfather being murdered – but at the same time, she realized what an odd claim it was.

I asked her, "You said, you *think* your grandfather was murdered. That means you're not sure?"

"Yes," she admitted, gripping and ungripping her hands. Then she sat up straight, determined.

"But I can't leave things that way. Sort of in-between. I've got to know. One way or another, I need to know."

She leaned toward me, her eyes zeroing in on mine.

"Please help me, Mr. Jonas. I've been to the police, but they say they can't do anything. I spoke with a Detective Charles Black. And he said you might be able to help. Can you, Mr. Jonas? Can you help me?"

Could I turn down a plea like that? From this...yeah, I'll say it... "damsel in distress?" Especially since she was referred by my former partner on the Job and longtime friend, L.A. Homicide Detective Charlie Black, who worked out of the Devonshire Station in Northridge.

If Charlie gave Ms. Morris my name, then it just might be that he saw something in what she said, to at least be worth some more attention. Not enough for him to open an official investigation, but enough for me to do some checking.

"Okay," I assured her, "Let's take a closer look."

"Thank you." She smiled, and relaxed a bit.

I smiled back.

"First though, let's do away with the formal stuff. Please call me, Will. And can I call you, Allison?"

"I prefer...Ally."

"Then Ally it is."

From a drawer in my desk, I took out my pad, ready to take notes. An old habit from my LAPD days, whenever I started a new homicide investigation. Inside secret: I really didn't need the pad and pencil – my memory isn't photographic, but close to it. So why the props? Because it made the folks I was interviewing feel that I was serious about helping them.

"First question," I started my interview of Ally, "when did your grandfather die?"

"A year ago. Last June. At the retirement and assisted living home where Grandpa was. On Winnetka. In Northridge. It's called 'Vistas'. He'd been there for about six months. Ever since

2

his health started failing. Also, because of the dementia he was beginning to experience. It became too much for my grandmother to take care of him at home, so we had to put him into the assisted living place."

"Do you know the details of his death?"

"He died during the night. One of the attendants told us he was worried about Grandpa. He hadn't been feeling well, earlier in the evening, so the attendant went to Grandpa's room at about 2 AM, to check on him. And that's when he found him. Dead. The attendant called the doctor who was on standby that night, he came right over, but there was nothing to be done. They called me. I went to the home and did the formal identification."

"How old was your grandfather?"

"Seventy-two."

I thought to myself, that's not so "old" nowadays. Hey, maybe I was thinking a bit defensively? Since I'm 59 – and that's only 13 years younger? Perish those thoughts, Will!

Back to my questioning Ally.

"You said his health started failing. What was the problem?"

"Mainly his heart. It was bad. The least bit of exertion, he'd get tired."

"How'd the doctor rule your grandfather's death?"

"He said grandpa's heart just gave out on him. He said the manner of death was natural. And the cause of death was heart failure. That's what he wrote on the death certificate."

I shook my head.

"I don't know, Ally. This looks pretty straightforward to me. Your grandfather had a weak heart, he wasn't feeling well, his heart failed, he died in his sleep, and the doctor ruled it death by natural causes. I don't see anything here that's out of line."

"Please, Will. I know the facts don't show it, but I believe my grandfather was murdered!"

"So you've said. But *why* do you believe that?"

"Because my grandmother told me so!"

"Because your grandmother told you so?"

"Yes! And I believe her. I believe my grandmother!"

Well, Folks, there you have it. How could I not believe Grandma?

This one was getting odder and odder. But…I'd told Ally that

3

I'd try and help, so I went on to the next step.

"Okay," I told her, "I need to talk to your grandmother."

Ally's hands started in again, with that gripping and ungripping action.

"Ally," I repeated, "I need to talk to your grandmother."

"I...that's not possible."

"Why not?"

"Because my grandmother is...dead. She died...last month."

CHAPTER TWO

Fact: Ally's grandmother told Ally her husband – Ally's grandfather – had been murdered.

Fact: But Ally's grandmother was dead – so there was no way to question her, about her claim.

Fact: But does this stop a determined investigator like yours truly? Read on.

"Okay," I said to Ally, "I want you to tell me, in detail, about your talk with your grandmother. When she told you your grandfather had been murdered in the assisted living home."

Six Weeks Earlier

"Is that better, Bubbe?" Ally addressed her grandmother – Deborah – with the Yiddish term. "Does the tea help to settle things?"

They were in Deborah's apartment in Chatsworth on Variel, just south of Devonshire. They were in the living room, Deborah in her lounging chair, Ally seated on the chair's edge.

Her grandmother sipped the tea and managed a weak smile.

"Having you visit is the best medicine, Darling."

Deborah placed the teacup on an adjacent end table and took both of Ally's hands in hers. Her smile faded, and her lips tightened.

Ally noticed the change and was concerned.

"Bubbe, what is it? What's the matter?"

Her grandmother didn't answer immediately. Then, she sighed, gathered her strength, and addressed her granddaughter.

"I'm not sure I should tell you...what I want to tell you. But I feel I must...before...

before I leave you. Before I die."

"Bubbe! You're not going to die!"

Deborah patted Ally's hands.

"If there is anything the cancer is making me sure about, my dearest Ally, it is...that I am going to die. And soon."

"Don't say that!"

"I must say it," Deborah insisted, "because there are things I need to tell you. Not things I want to tell you – but I must.

Because what happened to your grandfather, the way he died...was an injustice. And it needs to be corrected."

"I don't understand," Ally said.

"Allison...my Allison...I think...no...I am certain...that Zayde was killed. Yes, his heart was weak. Yes, his time was coming. But that time wasn't yet. When he died...it was because he was killed."

"How can that be? How can you know that?"

"It has to do with the camp. The concentration camp that Zayde was in, from 1942 until the camp was liberated in 1945."

"You mean Auschwitz?"

"Yes."

"Zayde never talked about that," Ally said. "Whenever I asked him, he wouldn't talk about it."

"Not to you. And for the most part, not to me, either."

Deborah took a sip of her tea.

"But in the few months before he went into the assisted living place, when we both knew the dementia was starting to affect him, Abe told me he had to talk to me. He told me he could no longer keep everything bottled up – inside him. He said, that before his memory left him, he had to admit to the truth. That he could not...as he put it...go to his grave without admitting — the terrible things he did, in order to survive."

Deborah took another sip of her tea.

"And he said, he was afraid, that if some people who were with him in Auschwitz...if they knew he was talking about what he – and they — did in there – they would want to silence him. To...kill him."

"What was he remembering? Who were those people?"

"He said there were three of them, and himself. They were all friends before the War. And they managed to stay together, in the same barracks in the camp. And what they did – well, he said some things. Not much. It was so hard for him to admit them. To talk about them. He said they would watch for anyone in the barracks who looked like they were going to die during the night. And they'd wait until everyone was asleep, and then they would take that person's belongings. Anything that was worth anything. Even if the person was still alive, but too weak to protest. And with the food, too. If someone seemed like they were dying, they would steal their food."

"Oh my god," Ally said.

"And he said there was more, too. After the camp. But he was too ashamed, he said, to tell me. I asked him. I kept asking him—what more, Abe, what more? But he wouldn't tell me."

"But what he *did* tell me, was that he was sure the three others would kill him, if they knew he was remembering...and talking."

"Grandma, this is so hard to believe. These things Zeyde told you?"

Deborah put her hands on Ally's shoulders and looked intently at her granddaughter.

"Ally, Ally...don't be too hard on Grandpa. Do we know...what *we* might have done? Just to stay alive, in that awful place? Would we have done differently?"

Ally returned her grandmother's stare.

"I...I don't know."

"Well, know this, My Ally. When your Grandfather told me these things, I could see his suffering. And I forgave him. I told him I understood. And I forgave him."

Deborah sighed.

"But I'm not sure he knew what I was saying to him. The dementia that let him remember those awful times 60 years ago in Auschwitz...well, it was also making it impossible for him to think clearly in the present time."

Deborah leaned toward Ally.

"One more thing I need to tell you. After he was already living in the assisted living home, Grandpa told me that he was being visited by the other three people who had been with him in Auschwitz. They were coming. One at a time. Always coming."

"But when I asked him – did he talk to them about what they did in in the camp? Did he tell them anything? He couldn't remember if he did — or didn't — say anything to them. But he kept repeating...to me...that they would kill him, if they knew what he was remembering. They would kill him. To keep him quiet."

Deborah paused and squeezed Ally's hands for emphasis.

"You know what I think, Ally? I think your grandpa *did* say something to one of those men. About remembering. And so they killed him. They killed my Abe. I know it. Zayde didn't just die because his heart gave out. He died because one of those people killed him."

Ally looked at me.

"That's all I have. I know it's not much. But I believe my grandmother was right. That my grandfather was murdered. And I need you to find his murderer."

I reviewed the conversation Ally had with her grandmother, and asked her, "Did your grandfather tell your grandmother the names of the three other people?"

"She said he couldn't remember their names. He remembered *them*, but not their names. But grandma did know who one of the men was. Because Grandpa and that man were business partners for a few years, so she got to know him. And she knew that the two of them were together in Auschwitz. And had also been friends before the concentration camp."

"Do you have his name?"

"Grandma said it was Irving Sherman."

"And the name of the company in which he and your grandfather were partners?"

"Elite Trucking. I looked them up. They're still in business. They're on Canoga Avenue in Canoga Park."

As I was adding that information to my notes, Ally asked, "Are you going to see him? See Sherman?"

"Not right away. Can't just waltz in there, and ask him if he killed your Grandpa. Don't think that would be too productive."

"Sorry. Dumb of me to ask."

"No. It's a legitimate question. And I am going to see Sherman eventually. But only when the timing is right."

I changed topics.

"In the meantime, I need to know how I can reach you."

Ally searched in her handbag, came out with a card case, and handed me a card that read: Allison Morris…Account Executive…Shadow Productions

And then an address in Studio City, along with the necessary phone, email and fax numbers.

"What's Shadow Productions?" I asked.

"We produce films, videos, presentations –for companies to use — as sales tools with their clients and new business prospects."

8

"Okay," I assured Ally, getting up from my desk, "I'll be back to you in a few days, with an update."

CHAPTER THREE

After Ally Morris left, I called Rose into my office.

She came marching in – Rose never walks, she marches – in sensible, soft-soled, low cut, lace up shoes. As she came in, I thought back to the day that I hired this 60-plus, gray-hair-tied-in-back, short and round lady who'd been with me for over seven years now, doing anything and everything that I needed done.

That day, I was hoping to hire my first assistant, to handle the office paperwork that was starting to pile up, as I got more assignments. I'd seen a half dozen ladies the employment agency had sent over, but no one was right for the job.

I was tired, and sitting at my desk, wondering what I was going to do about the situation, when Rose, a last minute referral from the agency, arrived.

"You look like hell," were her first words. "Stay there. Don't move," she ordered.

And then she made me the best cup of coffee I'd had in almost five years, ever since my wife, Vera, had died.

Of course, I hired her. Actually, I think Rose hired herself. Makes no difference, though. We've been together ever since.

"Nu?" she asked me now, "A new case?"

"Remember a few years ago, those Wildman grandchildren, who came in, with their dead grandmother's diary…"

"…Where she wrote that she killed her husband?" Rose finished my sentence. She often does that. Nothing shy about Rose.

"So? What now," she continued, "Another dead grandparent?"

"Yes, another dead grandparent."

"And the young one who just left – that has to be the granddaughter."

"Your powers of observation are amazing," I kidded her.

"At least I don't need to wear glasses when I read," Rose zinged me back.

And yeah, as was usually the case when we had these back and forth insult games – she battered me on this one. I had just started wearing reading glasses, which aggravated me. Not big time. But just enough to bring up that disturbing thought I'd been having more often nowadays… I'm getting old. I'm 59.

And just like every other time I thought about aging, I said my mantra, starting with my personal statistics. Still six four. Still 210 pounds. Still working out regularly. This led to my reassuring myself that I really wasn't that old. And once reassured, I got back to doing something useful – like filling Rose in, on the details of the case.

Then, I told her what I needed.

"Look up a company called Elite Trucking. They're on Canoga Avenue in Canoga Park. Maybe they've got a website? More companies seem to have them, now. Anyway, what I'm looking for, is a history of the company. Especially since the end of World War Two."

"And information on two men connected with the company. One is named Irving Sherman. The other is Abraham Levy. Ally told me that Sherman is still with the company. Levy is the dead – supposedly murdered — grandparent in this case. Sherman and Levy were partners in the business."

"Also, get me some background on the World War Two concentration camp, Auschwitz. I know the general stuff, but I'd like more details about day-to-day conditions."

"An uncle of mine was a survivor of that camp," Rose said. "His wife, his three children, both sets of grandparents – all killed."

"I…I'm sorry. Did you know your uncle?"

"As much as you could know someone who never really recovered. He was my father's younger brother. My parents brought him here. After the War. He lived with us."

Rose shook her head.

"But it was so sad. He didn't talk much. He never would go out by himself. He…he was afraid of everything. He only lived for a few years. It was like he didn't want to live. He had given up. And so he died. So sad…"

Rose looked at me, the concern clear on her face.

"This case…what you told me about it…what those people did to others, in the camp… makes me uncomfortable. I'm sorry, but it does."

"What do you mean?

"I mean, digging up those terrible details about how some

11

prisoners survived. What good does that do anyone? If I had been in Auschwitz, would I have acted differently than they did? Trying every way I could, to live? To survive? I...I can't blame any of them. I just can't"

I thought about what Rose said. Up until right now, I hadn't thought about the case in that way. Maybe it had something to do with the fact that Rose was Jewish, and I wasn't? She could feel Auschwitz. Hell...she had family ties to it. I sure didn't.

But then I reminded myself of one fact, and I answered Rose.

"I can understand what you're saying. And if it was just a matter of not talking about what a few people...not most people...what a few people did to survive – I could see – I could agree – to walk away from this case."

"But what we have here, Rose, is a possibility that an old man was murdered, just because, in his dementia, he was talking about what had happened. And if that's the case, and he was murdered, then this has to be investigated. And the killer has to be found. That's the way I look at it."

Rose nodded.

"You're right, of course. To kill a camp survivor. Someone who had already suffered so much. *That* is truly evil."

She picked up her pad and pencil.

"So what else do you need from me?"

"Just one more thing for now. A rundown on a retirement and assisted living place called 'Vistas.' It's on Ingomar in Winnetka."

When Rose left to do her research, I called my ex-partner, Charlie Black, a homicide detective in the LAPD station on Devonshire in Northridge.

"You're calling about Ally Morris and her dead grandfather," Charlie said, after my hello. "I just know it."

"You are so sharp," I kidded him back. "You should be a police detective."

"I am – on Mondays, Wednesdays and Fridays."

"Then I guess I'm lucky, today being Wednesday."

"I guess you are."

Charlie turned serious.

"So, Will...what do you think?"

"I think Ally is sincere. But this one might be a blank,

12

Charlie. I mean, all we have is the word of an old and sick – and now dead — lady, as to what her demented husband was remembering, about things that happened 60 years ago."

"But maybe, just maybe, Will…" Charlie prompted.

"And that's why you sent her over to me, right? Because you think there might be something there?"

"Just a hunch. Not anything I can do about it, here. So I figured you could poke around. You never know…"

"You never do," I agreed. "And I did tell Ally I'd investigate."

"Good."

I thought ahead a bit.

"Charlie, I may need some help from you. Don't know what, yet. Maybe access to some files? You okay with that?"

"Yup. No problem. Just as long as I can keep Klinger from knowing about it."

Captain Klinger was in charge of the LAPD station in Northridge. A strictly by-the-book cop. The kind that used to drive Charlie and me nuts, when I was still on the Job, and we were partners.

Let me explain. Our way of operating was simple, when chasing the bad guys. It was okay to cut a corner here and there – as long as we generally operated by the rules. But we were not "dot the I and cross the T" kinds of cops. And Klinger was.

"We'll worry about that one, if it ever comes up," I said.

"Agreed."

CHAPTER FOUR

I smelled the meatloaf as soon as I opened the door of the Tarzana condo, where my wife, Lu, and I lived. Got home a bit early. Lighter than usual traffic cut the drive time down to just 15 minutes from my office in Warner Center in Woodland Hills.

"The Master arrives," said the beautiful woman to whom I'd been married now for four years, as she came out of the kitchen and down the hall, to greet me.

And beautiful she was. At least in my view.

At 44, the former Lucy McClellan was tall – five feet nine inches in her stockinged feet. About136 well distributed pounds. Deep red hair. An angular face with a model's high cheek bones. And a perfect nose.

"Meat loaf?" I asked. "The next experiment in your rapidly growing list of main dishes you're learning to cook?"

About a year ago, Lu decided we needed to eat at home more often.

As she explained it to me, "We need to have less of that nasty restaurant conglomeration of whatever foods they so daintily arrange on an oversized plate, and for which we pay a fortune, every time we go out. We need to eat more, at home."

This was a noble thought, I told her, except for the fact that – and I tried to put this as nicely as I could... "You can't even make a good scrambled egg, remember?"

At which point Lu showed me a very large cookbook. Obviously new, with several hundred pages.

"Not to worry. The clerk in the store said I'd be able to cook anything properly, and tastefully, just by following the directions in this book."

And you know what? Lu was more right than wrong, with tonight turning out to be one of those "right nights." I love meatloaf. Nothing fancy about me. I was one satisfied husband.

"*That* was one helluva meatloaf," I told her.

I picked up my glass of club soda. Yeah, club soda. I'm a recovering alcoholic. Been clean for seven years now. I don't make a big deal out of it, but I thought you ought to know.

"A toast to the chef. May you make many more meat loafs in the years to come."

"Don't get too tied to that one dish, Will. I've got at least two dozen more main dishes I want to try and make."

"I'm ready. Just bring them on."

Lu laughed.

"You're in a good mood tonight. Something special happen today?"

"Not really. But it was an interesting day. Got a new client. Kind of an odd case."

"Tell me about it, can you?"

"Sure," I answered, and I gave Lu a rundown on my meeting with Ally Morris.

When I finished, Lu said, "I believe the grandmother. No doubt. Her husband was murdered."

"Come on, Lu. How can you say something like that? From what I told you? You're not being logical."

"Not logical? I'll give you that. But something is telling me, that the grandmother is right."

"Lu, you're a computer maven, right?"

My wife was the top computer programmer in a large, multi-office bank headquartered in Glendale.

"So?"

"So how can you rely on...to use your words... 'something is telling me' ...as a reason for believing dear old Grandpa was murdered? You? A computer expert? A believer in logic and technology?"

Instead of answering me, Lu carefully folded her napkin. Then, she got up and slinked – yes, slinked – over to me. She bent, and put her arms around my neck. Then she leaned in close to my face, so that her breasts crowded my lips. She whispered into my ear.

"So which do you prefer, Dear Man? My logic? Or this?" she asked, moving in ever closer.

"Mmmm..." was all I could manage, from where my face was buried.

But I do know one thing. At that moment, I definitely did not feel like 59.

CHAPTER FIVE

I spent the next morning in my office, working on assignments for some of my other clients.

One needed a plan for the best placement of cameras in his new warehouse, to discourage his products from doing a disappearing act.

Another client wanted a background check on a high level hire he was considering.

And then there's the one all PI's get stuck with some time, and hate: being retained by the suspicious wife, who wants her husband followed, for you-know-the-reason-why. This one, I subcontracted to another PI, who specialized in FCS...that is, follow, catch and snap.

After dealing with those clients, I went over the background information Rose had given me, about the concentration camp, Auschwitz, and about Vistas, the retirement and assisted living home where Abe Levy had been.

Didn't learn anything new in the general Auschwitz file. Just a renewed understanding of how awful the concentration camps had been.

As for Vistas, I did learn a few things.

First, unlike most of the operators of such places –which were national or regional chains — Vistas was an independent, small operation. A resident capacity of just 45.

And second, Vistas did not cater to the well-off folks whose happy faces you see in those advertisements. The typical Vista resident was middle or lower middle class, economically.

Time for a close-up look, I decided.

I called Rose in to my office and handed her the client files I'd been working on.

"These are all up to date, now," I told her.

I got up from my desk and took off my shoulder holster and weapon. I checked, to make sure my Glock 19 was on safety, then I put the holster and gun in the top right drawer of my desk. No need to carry a weapon today, I decided. Not for a visit to an old age home.

"I'm going to that retirement home, Vistas," I told Rose.

16

"Checking out your future home?" she asked.

"Not mine ... yours," I shot back.

And then I beat it out of the office, before Rose could counter attack.

Leaving my Warner Center office building in Woodland Hills, I took DeSoto north to Saticoy, then Saticoy east to Winnetka, then a few blocks north on Winnetka to Ingomar, where I turned right and spotted Vistas on my right.

The outside of the place confirmed my impression about Vistas' middle class status. The building was a plain brown and tan, one story. A parking lot took up most of the space in front. Landscaping was limited to grass lining the concrete path leading up to the front entrance. A porch ran the width of the building, with a few groupings of not-exactly-new, but still serviceable, plastic chairs, rockers and small tables.

I parked and went in. The lobby area was clean, decent looking, if not anywhere near new. It looked to me as if the operators of Vista were trying to make it a welcoming place.

There was a reception desk off to one side, and I headed toward it. Along the way, I was eyed by an old lady, seated on a nearby couch. She nodded, then visually followed me to the reception desk.

The receptionist smiled her smile.

"May I help you?" she asked.

"Hi," was my snappy reply. I handed her my card. "My name is Will Jonas. I'm a private investigator, and I'd like to talk to your manager, please. I need some information about a former resident here, a Mr. Abe Levy."

The receptionist looked at the card, then picked up her phone and dialed a number, at the same time saying to me, "I think the owner, Mr. Dworsky, would be the best person for you to talk with. I'll see if he is available."

As I waited for the receptionist to reach Dworsky, I noticed the old lady still looking at me and still smiling. What? Am I about to be picked up by a grandmother? I don't look that old, do I?

Just kidding. But the lady was smiling at me, so I smiled back.

No harm in that, right? Spreading some cheer among the

17

seniors?

"Please go down the hallway," the receptionist interrupted my eye-to-eye with grandma, "and Mr. Dworsky will be waiting for you."

At the end of the hallway, I was met by a shirt-sleeved man, who looked to be in his mid or late 40's, bald, a bit on the pudgy side, and with a smile.

"Mr. Jonas? I'm Ed Dworsky."

We shook hands, and Dworsky pointed toward his office. "Come in, please."

Once inside, Dworsky led me to a small couch, waited until I sat, and then joined me.

I handed him another of my cards.

"Thanks for seeing me," I said. "I'm looking for some information about a former resident of yours, Abe Levy. Died about a year ago. Manner: natural. Cause: heart failure."

Dworsky thought for a few seconds, then nodded.

"Yes, I remember. Early to mid-stage dementia. Also a weak heart."

"Good memory," I complimented him.

"Well, we try to treat our residents as people, not just numbers or bodies. So, I tend to remember them, even after they've passed. Now, what can I do for you?"

It was time for my spiel.

To explain, I knew, going in, that most places like this, don't like to give out too much information about their clients. Good idea, actually. But I needed information, so I had prepared what you might call, my opening statement, or spiel. Here's hoping it works.

"I'm here as a representative of the Abraham Levy family," I told Dworsky. "You probably don't know it, but Mr. Levy's wife died about a month ago."

"Sorry to hear that. I remember her, too. She visited her husband frequently. I knew that she had cancer. Was that the cause of her death?"

"Yes. And now here's the situation. My client is the Levy's granddaughter, Allison Morris. You may remember her. She also visited Mr. Levy. Anyway, she's the executor of the estate. Not much of an estate, financially. But Allison has found some old pictures in her grandmother's files, along with written instructions from Mr. Levy."

"The instructions are – that when they're both dead – the pictures should be distributed to – as Mr. Levy wrote – 'his friends from Auschwitz.'"

"Auschwitz? The World War Two concentration camp?" Dworsky asked.

"Yes. According to what the grandmother had told her granddaughter, Mr. Levy and three other men were close friends in the camp. And for some reason, no one knows why, Mr. Levy wanted the pictures given to them. They look like pictures taken after the War, in one of the displaced persons camps. Group shots of the four of them. As I said, no one can figure out – why – Mr. Levy wanted the others to have the shots. But it evidently was important to him. And now, his granddaughter would like to honor his request. Especially since it involves such an important part of his life. His survival of Auschwitz."

I paused for emphasis.

"The problem is, though, no one knows the names of these friends."

Dear Reader...of course, you and I know that I do have one of the names...an Irving Sherman, with whom Abe Levy had been partners at one time in Elite Trucking.

But I didn't want to share this information with Dworsky, because if Sherman was one of the men Levy felt was threatening to kill him...well, I didn't want to bring his name into the conversation, until I had a chance to check him out.

"No one knows their names?" Dworsky asked for confirmation. "That's odd."

"Yes it is," I agreed. "But as Allison explained it to me, her grandfather first began talking about his experiences in Auschwitz – only when he was starting to be affected by the dementia. Before then, he had never wanted to talk about the camp. Not to his wife. Not to his granddaughter. Not to anyone."

"That's not at all unusual," Dworsky said. "One of the facts about dementia is that the patient may remember long ago events."

"That's what we figure. Mr. Levy did start to talk about his experiences. And he did mention his three friends. But he just never named them."

I leaned toward Dworsky for emphasis.

"And that's why I'm here today, Mr. Dworsky. Allison is hoping that maybe, while he was here, her grandfather continued to talk about the camp. And maybe he mentioned the names of his friends. Possibly to one of the attendants? Perhaps the one who found him that evening when he died? We understand that person may have been close to Mr. Levy? Or perhaps the doctor who signed the death certificate? I've seen a copy. It's a Dr. Amos Clayton, right? Perhaps I could see both of them, if that would be okay with you?"

"Also, Allison did tell me that her grandmother told her, that Mr. Levy mentioned some friends coming to visit him, while he was here. We're hoping they might be the friends from Auschwitz, that Mr. Levy kept referring to. The people who should get the pictures. Your visitors do have to sign in, don't they?"

Dworsky nodded.

"Yes, they do. As for the attendant, that probably would be Edwin Nesbitt. Doctor Clayton, though, is no longer with us." Dworsky shook his head. "The man had a drinking problem. Managed to hide it for some time. But eventually, I had to let him go."

Then, Dworsky went silent, and I knew what he was thinking. Time to call his lawyer, to see if he could give me the information I was asking for. Well, I really didn't want to get into that kind of hassle. Because the lawyer would probably advise Dworsky to refuse my request for information. How'd I know that? Because that's what lawyers do. They say no...to just about everything.

It was time to play my ace card. I hoped it would be a winner.

I put on what I hoped was my maximum sincerity face. The best that I could give it.

"Please, Mr. Dworsky, I do understand that you may have some concerns, legally, about giving out information. And Ms. Morris also realizes this. So, she has instructed me to tell you, that she does not want to cause any concerns – or legal costs – for you. She said to tell you, that if you are uncomfortable about sharing this information, then just disregard her request."

I shook my head.

"She will simply forgo doing anything with the pictures. She had wanted very much to honor her grandfather's memory, especially as related to the awful experiences he and his friends had at Auschwitz – but if need be, she'll simply destroy the pictures, and that will be that."

Dworsky thought for a few seconds, then made up his mind.

"All right, when you put it that way, I don't see any problem in cooperating."

So, Folks, am I proud that my violin strings play on Auschwitz worked? No. But I need the information, so I can live with it.

Dworsky continued, "First off, about the attendant – I need to check the duty roster, but I'm pretty sure it would be Edwin Nesbitt."

"About the visitors to Mr. Levy, we'll have to search our visitor registration files to cover the time he was a resident. That will take a day or two."

"This is terrific," I said. "If I can see Nesbitt today, that would be very helpful."

"Okay," Dworsky said, standing up, "I'm going to put you in the small conference room next door. And I'll have Nesbitt come to you. It'll take a few minutes. Not sure exactly what he's doing at the moment."

Nesbitt came to the conference room about ten minutes later.

In his green medical pants and top, Nesbitt looked very much as I would have expected. He was in his mid-forties. Stood about five-nine, trim and in good shape. His handshake was firm. He had a poker face, hard to read anything, except for a bit of anxiety, but that was natural enough, under the circumstances.

I explained the purpose of my visit to Nesbitt, and then wound up with, "And so, what I'm hoping, is that maybe Levy mentioned some names to you? People he was with, in Auschwitz?"

Nesbitt thought a bit, then shook his head. "Mr. Levy did mention Auschwitz from time to time. He mainly called it, 'the camp.' And he did talk about his friends there. But never any names. He never mentioned any names."

"What about his visitors? I know, of course, that his granddaughter, Allison Morris, was one. And that until she was too sick to visit, his wife also came."

"Correct. They came regularly."

"Any other visitors? Especially, any older men? Men who might have been with him in the camp?"

Nesbitt nodded. "Yes. I think there were two or three."

"Know their names?"

"No. Mr. Levy never mentioned any of those names to me."

"Okay," I tried a different angle. "Just in general, you were around Levy a lot, right?"

"Yes. He was one of my primaries. One of the people I was responsible for."

"Did he ever mention any names? Maybe even just out of the blue? Maybe not seemingly connected to anything? Perhaps when he was having a bad day, dementia-wise?"

Nesbitt shook his head.

"Sorry. No. No names."

That was about it, with Nesbitt. He didn't have anything more to add, so our meeting ended.

After Nesbitt left, I went next door and looked into Dworsky's office. He was at his desk, reading a file spread out on his desk. I rapped on the open door to get his attention.

"Thanks for letting me see Nesbitt."

"Was he of any help?"

"Not too much. But it was useful to interview him. Also, I'm wondering...I can check other sources, but do you happen to know where Dr. Clayton went? After he left here?"

"No. Sorry, but I don't."

"Okay, then I'm pretty much done for now, except for the names of those visitors."

"I set someone on that already," Dworsky said. "I should be able to give you that information by tomorrow."

I left Dworsky's office, went down the hall, across the lobby and out the main entrance. And guess who was waiting for me out there? The lady in the lobby. My grandma "pickup," sitting in a chair to the right of the entrance.

"Young man," she called out when she saw me. And then she motioned me over, with the command presence of a marine drill sergeant.

Does this grandma have style? "Young man," she had called me. Okay, she must have been in her upper seventies or in her eighties –so to her, I was a young man. But let's not quibble.

"Ma'am, what can I do for you?" I asked her.

"Did you get the information you needed, about Abe Levy?"

"Some of it." And then I wondered. "Why do you ask? Did you know Mr. Levy?"

The lady nodded.

"Yes. Abe, and his wife, Deborah, were good friends of mine, for many years, before they ended up dead…and me here, on the way to being dead. And while Abe was here, he and I did a lot of talking together."

She stuck her hand out. "I'm Polly Gladstein."

"Will Jonas," I told her, as we shook hands.

"So, what kind of questions do you have about Abe? Maybe I can help?"

"Be great if you can. Here's the story. According to Abe's granddaughter, Abe kept talking to Deborah about three of his friends, from when they were in Auschwitz, during World War Two. I'm a private investigator, and I'm trying to help the granddaughter find those three, but Abe never told Deborah their names. He said he remembered the men, but he couldn't remember their names."

"So, did Abe ever talk with you, about having friends from when he was in Auschwitz?"

"Yes, he did."

"What did he say?"

"Much of it was just rambling. Because of the dementia. He kept talking about what he called 'the bad things' he and his friends did. And about the killing. The killing that no one ever knew about."

"What killing?" I asked Polly.

Polly shook her head.

"He never said. He just kept referring to…'The killing. The killing.'"

"Okay, what about names? Did Abe ever mention any names? And specifically, the names of those friends of his, that he kept referring to?"

"He did mention some names. I don't know if they're the names you're looking for. They were just names. He didn't describe them. Or say where he knew them from."

"Do you remember those names?"

Polly was insulted.

"Of course I remember the names. I don't have dementia! My body may be shriveling, but my mind, thank God, is still healthy. And I've always had a good memory."

I took out my pad and pencil.

"So can you please give me those names?"

"Okay, one of them was…Semanski."

"Another was…Fedorov."

"And the third one was…Beletski."

"What do you suppose those names are? Polish? Russian? Something else?"

"They're Polish."

"Any chance that you can spell them for me?"

Polly smiled.

"Of course. I still speak some Polish. From when I was a child. I'm from Poland, originally."

"Were you…in one of the concentration camps?"

Polly shook her head.

"No. My parents, God bless them…they were among the few smart ones who saw what was happening in Germany in the early 1930's…and what that would mean to the rest of Europe…and they emigrated to the United States."

"So, now the spelling of the names. Ready?"

I was, and Polly spelled them out for me.

"Semanski…S E M A N S K I."

"Fedorov…F E D O R O V."

"Beletski…B E L E T S K I."

"No first names?" I asked.

Polly shook her head.

"No first names."

Well, I thought to myself, hopefully the first names will show up on the Vista's visitor register that Dworsky was having checked.

I had another question for Polly.

"Aside from Mr. Levy's family did you ever see any of his visitors who might have been Semanski, or Fedorov or Beletski?"

"I did see some visitors. But what were their names? This, I don't know. This, I can't tell you."

"You've been very helpful," I said to Polly. "Tell me, is there anything I can do for you?"

Polly laughed.

"Only in my imagination. And it wouldn't be proper for an old lady like me to say any more."

On the way back to my office, some questions started creeping around inside my head.

Question number one: how come Polly Gladstein heard Abe Levy mention those three names of the guys who probably were his friends — but the attendant, Nesbitt, never heard the names? Odd, since Nesbitt spent plenty of time with Levy. I needed to talk to Nesbitt again.

Question number two: where was Doctor Clayton...the MD who signed Levy's death certificate? I wanted to talk to him, in case he had spent time with Levy, maybe giving him a periodic once-over, every month or two? Did Levy ever mention any names to him?

Question number three: what about Elite Trucking, the company in which Irving Sherman and Abe Levy had been partners? I needed to review the file Rose was putting together for me on Elite. It probably was ready by now. Rose had been working on it, when I left the office, earlier.

Question number four: was it time yet to set up a meeting with Louis the Fisherman? No, not that kind of fisherman. Louis was not interested in cod, or tuna, or halibut. What did interest him was...information. The kind that cops – or PI's -- can use, when tracking someone or something. Information that Louis was an expert at finding...in ways that I never wanted to know about. More about Louis, later.

CHAPTER SIX

Once I was back in my office, I called Lu, at work – at the bank in Glendale where she was the head programmer.

"What's the matter, Will," she asked. "You calling to tell me you won't be home for dinner? I thought I was making real progress in my cooking."

"You are, Lu. You are. And I will be home for dinner. But I have something I'd like to you to take a crack at."

"You mean, work my computer magic for you?"

"Yup."

"Like...look up some files? Or heaven forbid, maybe even hack into some?"

"No details, please. You know I don't understand that stuff."

"You mean, you don't *want* to understand. You just want the results."

"Something like that. Yes."

Lu laughed.

"Okay, what do you need?"

"I'm going to give you three last names. Surnames. And I'm hoping you can locate where these people are." I spelled the names out for Lu:

SEMANSKI

FEDOROV

BELETSKI."

I continued, "I'm told they're Polish surnames. And I'm trying to track down if these are the people who visited Abe Levy in that retirement home. Because if they are, then they may be the men that Levy believed would kill him.

"So, it would be great, Lu, if you could figure out a way to see if these are the same men who were friends with Levy, when they all were together in Auschwitz during World War Two. I don't figure there is anything you can do about the time in Auschwitz. But maybe there's a way to check to see if these men came to the United States after World War Two. Probably in 1945 or 1946. More than likely, they came in as displaced persons, and arrived via New York. Their ages probably between high teens to low twenties."

"You're making a lot of assumptions, Will."

"Yeah, I know. But it's all I have to go on, right now. And while we're at it, here's another assumption –another guess – on my part. It's also possible that, at some point, they all may have changed their names – to make them more American sounding."

"Why do you think so?"

"Because I know that Abe Levy's partner in a company called Elite Trucking was a man named, 'Irving Sherman.' And if it turns out that Sherman and Levy were friends back at Auschwitz, then that person's name may well have been that first name I gave you – Semanski."

"I mean, changing from Semanski to Sherman is a nice switch. It's an Americanization that would make sense. At least, I'm hoping it makes sense."

"And as long as we're on this name-changing point, I'm feeling pretty good about this assumption of mine. I remember, back in high school, a friend of mine was named Eddie Block. Only he told me that his family's original name – back in Poland – was Blaharsky. But his grandfather changed it to Block, when he got to the U.S."

"So name changing is not that far out, I don't think."

"We'll find out," Lu agreed.

"Will, this is going to take some deep searching. Immigration records, to try and track down those names as being of persons coming into the country. And court records, to see if they became citizens. And county clerk records to see if any of them changed their names. Probably some census records, too. Also, given the advanced ages of these people, a search of social security records would be a good idea, to see if they are still alive. And to top it off, if I do find them – let's say, initially in New York — well, we're here in Los Angeles. So I may have to do some multiple state searching."

"Any idea how long it's going to take?"

"At least a few days. I'm jammed with bank work right now, too. So I'm going to do this over the next couple of evenings."

"Rose," I called out, after Lu and I were finished.

Rose marched in a few seconds later.

"Good lungs, but you could also buzz me, you know."

27

"I prefer to call," was my reply.

"Whatever…" Rose said dismissively, using that word with just as much effect as any teenager could hope for, when downsizing a parent.

She handed me a several page computer printout.

"I assume you hollered, because you wanted this? The file I put together on Elite Trucking."

"Yes. Thanks. Anything interesting in there? Anything hit you?"

"No. Looks pretty straightforward."

"While I'm going through it, see if you can locate a Doctor Amos Clayton. He used to work for Vistas, but he was canned within the last year because they said he had a drinking problem. He's the doc who signed Abraham Levy's death certificate, and I want to talk to him."

Rose sighed.

"What's the matter?" I asked.

"That poor Mr. Levy," she said. "If it does turn out that he was killed."

She shook her head.

"To have survived Auschwitz…and then to be killed before his time. It's not right. It's just not right."

Rose left, and I started looking at the Elite file.

First off, there it was – Irving Sherman – listed as president. According to Ally Morris, Sherman was Abe Levy's partner, before they split up, and also was one of the four original friends at Auschwitz.

Elite was founded in 1945, right after the end of World War Two, by a Richard Kohn. Its customers were small and medium sized companies, that used Elite to ship goods to cities in the Western and Central United States.

In 1961, Kohn died, and Sherman and Levy bought the company from Kohn's wife, who had inherited it. Financing was conventional, through a bank, and the loan was paid off by 1966.

Sherman and Levy had both joined Elite in 1946, initially as warehouse clerks, then in the office, as they worked their way up the small staff. Before they bought Elite, Sherman had been vice president, and Levy was manager of operations.

Sherman bought out Levy's partnership in 1966, it looked like right after they had paid off their joint loan to the bank. I wondered why. Why did Levy leave what looked to be a successful, nice sized business? Anything to do with that bond of silence, that he, Sherman and the other two men had sworn, as regards what they had done in Auschwitz? Any increasing strain starting to be felt? Certainly, something to wonder about, and to look at, further.

But now, it was time to set a meeting with Louis The Fisherman. Let me explain who Louis is. To put it in its simplest terms...Louis is an informant, a snitch. Someone who uncovers bad things about people and things. And then sells that information to the police. Or to people like me – a former cop who used Louis for information, when I was still on the Job.

I had used Louis a number of times over the years. For a hefty fee, he usually delivered the information I wanted. And sometimes, even information I didn't know I needed, until Louis gave it to me.

Some usual things about Louis.

First, most snitches have a short life span. But Louis is a survivor. Because he is super careful. And very smart. Probably has more "smarts" than most of his law enforcement clients, including yours truly.

Second, Louis understands Economics. That is, he knows how to charge for what he has to sell. No penny ante kind of fee. Louis charges in the hundreds. And he gets it, because he delivers valuable information.

Okay, time to call Louis.

I dug out the three cell phone numbers I had for him, and tried the first one. Out of service. Not surprising. Louis keeps changing his cell phone numbers. Another survival tactic.

I tried the second number and there was a pickup at the other end. Nothing said, though. You had to know, that on calls like this, Louis did not talk. The caller needed to do the talking, needed to ID himself to Louis. So, I ploughed ahead.

"Louis, this is Will Jonas. Got some work for you. We need to meet. Let me know when and where."

I left my office and cell numbers, knowing that Louis would call me back – when he felt it was the right time to do so. When would that be? Who knew? I didn't. But I was sure he would call me, at some point, that was right for him.

CHAPTER SEVEN

The next day, I was in my office, when Rose told me that Ed Dworsky, the Vistas' owner, was calling. I picked up my phone.

"Mr. Dworsky," I said. "Hopefully you're calling with the names of those visitors to Abe Levy?"

"Yes, we went through the guest register, and we did find the names of Mr. Levy's visitors, including his wife and his granddaughter, and a few others that we recognized as friends and relatives."

"But aside from those?"

"We found three names that started appearing in the four months before Mr. Levy died. Three visits per name. The names were: Smith, Jones and West."

"Smith, Jones and West," I repeated. "Somehow, I get the feeling those are not real names."

"Well...to be honest with you, I've got the same feeling. A good number of our residents are, like Mr. Levy, Jewish. And their visitors tend, also, to be Jewish. You know. Family and close friends."

"And Smith, Jones and West just don't cut it, in that way," I said.

"I would have to agree. I...I'm sorry. Perhaps we should be more vigilant about our sign-in procedures..."

"Don't beat yourself up," I said, "You're running a retirement home, not a high security military base."

"Again, I'm sorry. If there is anything I can do..."

After Dworsky's call, I did some thinking –sometimes dangerous on my part – but sometimes productive.

First thing to note. There *had* been some visits to Levy by persons unknown. At least 9 visits in four months. I tagged these as "unknowns," because the names, Smith, Jones and West just didn't figure right.

There was also the possibility, of course, that one person did all nine visits, and used all three names. But I didn't see any reason for this, so I put it down as a very low probability.

Second, it looked to me, that by spreading the visits over four months, the visitors were trying to monitor Levy's dementia, to see if it was getting worse. And to see if, as a result of the worsening, Levy was talking more about what they did in Auschwitz.

Third, was it reasonable to believe that the Smith, Jones and West trio were his friends from Auschwitz? Very reasonable, in my book.

Fourth, could it be that the Smith-Jones-West visitor sign-ins actually were named Semanski-Fedorov-Beletski – the names Polly Gladstein had heard Levy mention?

Fifth, was it time for me to visit someone I already knew *was* one of those friends — Irving Sherman, el numero uno at Elite Trucking? No. Not yet, something told me. Hold off, for now.

And sixth, just to be on the safe side, I needed to review the Semanski-Fedorov-Beletski name's with Ally Morris. Hey, maybe they *were* just regular friends of her grandfather. Nothing to do with Auschwitz. I doubted it, but I needed to check.

"Smith, Jones and West? Those names aren't familiar to me," Ally said, when I called her at her office. "I never heard my grandfather, or my grandmother, mention those names."

"Okay, I've got three more names for you. These are names that one of the residents at Vistas – someone who was friendly with your grandfather – said your grandfather mentioned. She couldn't tell me anything more about them – just that your grandfather did mention them. They are: Semanski, Fedorov and Beletski."

I spelled them out, and then asked, "What about these names? They mean anything to you?"

After a few seconds, Ally answered, "No. Sorry. I don't think I've ever heard those names. Do you know anything about them?"

"Not yet. I'm working on it," I told her.

Then another thought hit me.

"Ally, what about your grandfather? Was his name always Levy? Or did he change it from something else, when he got here?"

"As a matter of fact," Ally replied, "my grandfather did change it, my grandmother told me. His original name was...Levenbuk. Is this helpful to you?"

"Could be," I told her.

I figured this information might be helpful to Lu, in her search for the three Polish names, so I made a mental note to let her know.

Rose stuck her head into my office, and mouthed the words, "Louis The Fisherman," and then held an imaginary phone to her ear.

"Ally, I need to take this other call. Sorry. I'll be back to you, soon."

I cut the connection with Ally.

"Hello," I said, careful not to mention any name or to ID the person at the other end. That's the way Louis liked to have it.

I heard, "Tomorrow night. Seven PM. Westfield Shopping Center on Topanga. Park next to the elevator on the second floor, so your car is facing the Neiman Marcus north side entrance."

I heard a click, and the line went dead.

The Fisherman, of course. Our meeting was set for tomorrow night.

CHAPTER EIGHT

I had asked Rose to try and locate Dr. Amos Clayton, the doc who had signed Abe Levy's death certificate. The Vistas' owner, Dworsky, had said he let Clayton go, the man liked his alcohol too much, but Dworsky didn't have any forwarding address for Clayton.

Rose found what looked to be a home address for the doctor. Nothing about any present professional affiliations, however.

So, the next morning, after ploughing through some necessary office paperwork I decided it was time to talk to the good doctor. My hope was that he might remember something useful, that Abe Levy may have said. Maybe some more names? Or more details about the three Polish names we did have? Or something about Auschwitz?

The address for Dr. Clayton was on Odessa, in Van Nuys. From my office, I took the 101 Freeway east, then the 405 north. I exited at Victory Boulevard, took Victory east to Odessa, turned left on Odessa for a couple of blocks, and there it was...a two story apartment building at 16735, the address Rose had given me. It was a small, plain building. Not exactly what I expected as the home digs of an MD.

I parked, locked my car, and walked up to the building's entrance. There was an entry pad, with the names of the residents on it. I pushed the button for Clayton, in apartment 1G, and after a few seconds, a woman answered.

"Who is this?" she asked.

"Hello. I'm looking for Dr. Amos Clayton."

There was a short pause, and then the woman said, softly, "He...died six months ago."

Not an answer I expected. But I had a hunch it was an answer about which I'd like more details. Time to move carefully, though.

"I'm so sorry. I didn't know."

I guessed, "Is...this...Mrs. Clayton?"

"Yes. Who are you?"

"My name is Will Jonas, Mrs. Clayton. I'm a private investigator. And about a year ago, your husband signed the death certificate of a Mr. Abraham Levy, a resident of the Vistas

MANIFESTO/YOU REMEMBER... YOU DIE

retirement home. On behalf of Mr. Levy's family, I've been checking about some of the circumstances of Mr. Levy's life at the home in the months preceding his death. And I was hoping to talk to Dr. Clayton, because of his role as the attending physician."

No response from the other end, so I pushed on.

"Mrs. Clayton, can I spend a few minutes with you? It might be helpful to my investigation."

"I don't see how."

"Just a few minutes," I repeated. "I'd really appreciate it."

After a few silent seconds, during which I sensed I shouldn't do any more pushing,
the buzzer sounded. I went in, and walked down the hall, to apartment 1G, which was at the rear
of the building. When I reached the apartment, I rang the bell, and after a couple of beats, the
door opened.

The woman who opened it looked like she was in her mid or late fifties. Medium height. Medium build. Her face held traces of what must have been very attractive features when she was a young woman. Plainly, but neatly dressed.

"Mrs. Clayton?" I asked, holding out one of my cards.

She took the card, glanced at it, and then stepped aside to let me in.

"Please sit down," she said, inviting me into the small living room.

In keeping with the building's exterior, the room was plain, very ordinary. The furniture was old, but everything was neat and clean and nicely put together. And it seemed to me that Mrs. Clayton – despite her husband's death, and what must have been a hard life, married to an alcoholic, hadn't yet given up the good fight, to try and live decently. I was glad to see it. She seemed like a nice person who deserved something better.

"You're lucky to have found me in," she said. "I'm usually at work by now. But I'm on the late shift today."

"What kind of work is that?"

"I'm a sales person at Ruby's Housewares," she said, mentioning a chain outfit that had outlets throughout southern California.

"Now," she continued, "what's this, about your investigating someone's death, with Amos having signed the death certificate?'"

"Your husband didn't do anything wrong," I assured her. "Everything's in order on the death certificate for Mr. Levy. What I'm looking for, is some information that Doctor Clayton may have had, about Mr. Levy."

Before I got to that point, I was curious about the doctor's death, so I asked, "You said your husband died six months ago? Can I ask – what was the cause?"

Mrs. Clayton gave a deep sigh.

"The cause? He was drunk, he fell asleep in an alley, and he was run over. By a hit and run."

"Wow," was my surprised reply.

"Yes, wow," Mrs. Clayton, echoed.

She shook her head.

"Just another low point, after a high point, in the life of my poor, alcoholic husband."

It was clear to me that Mrs. Clayton, even though she may not have realized it, was looking for a sympathetic ear. And I was ready to provide it. Both because I felt for the lady. And because – okay, I'll admit it – I was hoping I might learn something useful.

"I don't get the low point-high point reference," I said.

Mrs. Clayton was silent for a short while, her face angled toward the floor. Then, she looked up at me.

"There were times, when Amos would try and stay off the alcohol – and he would succeed for a while. Those times were always the high points."

"Another high point was about a year ago, when Amos was still working at Vistas – and he came home with $5,000, and gave it to me. He said one of the patients, with no heirs, had left it to him in her will, and she had just died."

"And then again, just a few weeks before he was killed, he brought me another $5,000. Said another patient had died and left it to him."

"Each of those $5,000 amounts was a high point, helping me to catch up with most of our debts."

Mrs. Clayton paused, bit her lip, and then looked at me with some intensity.

"Look, Mr. Jonas, these high points I'm talking about? I've given them nice labels in my own mind. But I'm no fool. Two

36

patients? Each leaving Amos $5,000? Not very likely."

She shrugged. "Well," she continued, "among his many talents, Amos was a gambler. A good poker player, when he was sober. So I figured he won the money, playing cards. I didn't say anything to him, though. God help me, I didn't really want to know the source of the money. Both times, we needed it. And so I didn't say anything. Didn't ask him for any explanation."

"I understand," I sympathized. Then I switch topics. "Any witnesses to the hit and run?"

"No."

"Where did it happen?"

"Up in Chatsworth. In the parking lot of a Mexican restaurant. I think the name is, 'El Amigo.'"

I knew the place. It was on Devonshire, a few blocks west of Mason. Good restaurant. Busy bar.

"That's at least 15 miles from here," I said. "Did your husband usually go so far away, when he was out drinking?"

Mrs. Clayton shook her head.

"No. He usually went to two bars, here in the neighborhood. Places where they knew him. Where the bartenders would, if necessary, call me, and I would come and collect him, and bring him home. Why he went drinking up in Chatsworth, this time, I just don't know."

I asked, "How'd he get there, I wonder? Did your husband usually drive, when he was drinking?"

Mrs. Clayton laughed, but there was no humor in it.

"Did he drive? No, he couldn't. There was no car *to* drive. It had been repossessed."

She shook her head again.

"I loved that man, Mr. Jonas. Through it all, I loved him."

I couldn't help thinking, sometimes Life is a real ball breaker.

"Mrs. Clayton, I'm truly sorry for your loss. I wish it could have been different."

She smiled.

"Thank you." She straightened up on her seat. "Now, you said something about Amos possibly having some information about this patient, Mr. Levy?"

"Yes. We're trying to locate some old friends of the patient, and we were hoping that Mr. Levy may have mentioned some names to your husband. Just in any general conversations they may have had. So, did your husband ever say anything about his conversations with Mr. Levy?"

"No. Amos wasn't one to bring home much in the way of talk, about what happened during the day. Probably the result of the patient/doctor confidentiality motto that's drummed into them, starting in medical school."

"So the name, 'Abe Levy' never came up in conversation?"

"No. I don't recall ever having heard that name."

I stood up.

"That's about it," I told Mrs. Clayton. "I thank you for your time. And again, I'm sorry for your loss."

Mrs. Clayton walked me the front door.

"Sorry I've not been of any help," she told me. "If I think of anything, I certainly will let you know."

CHAPTER NINE

"Charlie, your hunch may have been right on target," I said to Charlie Black, when I called him at the Northridge Station that afternoon. "I'm beginning to think that there's something not too kosher about Abe Levy's death at Vistas."

"Tell me more," Charlie said.

"It's all circumstantial," I warned, "but interesting. Here's what I've found out.

"First, there's the doctor who signed the death certificate – Amos Clayton. His wife told me he received two, $5,000 cash payments. He told her, these were payments from the wills of grateful patients who had died. People he'd taken care of, while they were in Vistas. I got the feeling she didn't really believe him, as to the source of the payments. And it sounds wrong to me, too."

"What's really interesting here though, is the *timing* of the payments. One was about the time Levy died. And the second, Clayton received just before he was killed in a hit and run."

"Think about it, Charlie. Clayton signs the death certificate, attributing death to natural causes – and he gets that first five thousand."

"And then, about six months later, Clayton gets a second five thousand – and he dies right afterwards."

"So," Charlie said, "You're thinking that Clayton got $5K to declare Levy's death as being natural – when it might not have been. And then he got greedy, and demanded a second $5K. From someone. We don't know who. He got that second $5K. But then he was killed in a hit and run that's never been solved. In other words, the source, offed him."

"That's exactly what I'm thinking," I said. "The timing coincidences are too real to be ignored."

"Okay, let's go with that for right now. What else you got?" Charlie asked.

"The hit and run that killed Clayton. The circumstances there are kind of odd. The first thing to note is that Clayton, according to his wife, was an alcoholic. And that he stayed in the neighborhood to do his drinking. A couple of local bars. But, he was run over, in the parking lot of a bar in Chatsworth, a good 15 miles from where he lived. And Clayton didn't own a car. His wife told me it'd been repossessed."

"So, the questions are," Charlie said, "How come he was there, in Chatsworth? And how'd he get there?"

"Right. And there's some other stuff, too. At Vistas itself. Things that don't add up. Having to do with the staff attendant who was responsible for Levy, day-to-day. And some visits Levy was getting, from people signing the guest book with false names. These are leads I still need to run down."

"Will, I'm wondering if it's time for you to turn this over to LAPD."

"Charlie, I want to keep going on this a while longer. Like I said, what I've got is all circumstantial. Plus, there's more I'm working on. So, I want to stay on it, for now."

Charlie laughed.

"Why'd I even ask? I knew what your answer would be. But listen, timing is important here. Eventually, I'm going to have to take this to Klinger. And you know what his reaction is going to be, when he finds out I passed this off to you, in the beginning. I can handle that, up to a point – 'Captain...I just had a hunch. Not enough for us to warrant opening a formal investigation...tada...tada...tada.'

"Okay, that will fly – but only up to a point. Beyond that, I'll get my head handed to me, and not on a silver platter."

"Understood," I assured him.

"So keep me informed, Will. Keep me informed."

"I will."

"And now the key question," Charlie continued, "As you're making me these promises, do you have your fingers crossed behind your back? Because if you do..."

"No! My fingers are not crossed. So, my promise is real. I am not bullshitting you."

"Okay."

"But I do have one request," I said.

"No surprise. What is it?"

"I'd like a copy of the file on Dr. Clayton's hit and run."
"Okay, I can manage that."

CHAPTER TEN

The next evening, I drove north on Topanga Canyon Boulevard, cut a right on Kittridge into the Westfield Topanga shopping mall, followed the internal road around to the upramp for second story parking, drove up there, and then across to the far right corner of the parking area.

I parked in the space next to the elevator. Looking straight ahead, I could see theNeiman Marcus entrance, one story down.

I checked my watch. It was 7PM on the nose.

I looked at the elevator. The door opened and – no surprise – there was Louis.

He held the elevator door open, looked to his left, looked to his right, and then walked quickly to my car and got in.

"Drive out of here and head north on Owensmouth," he ordered. "Then we'll talk."

Genuine Louis, this was. All caution. All business. Well, can't blame the guy. It's how he's stayed alive much longer than the usual snitch number of years.

"The file in that envelope next to you," I said to Louis as I worked my way out of the mall, "is on a company here in the Valley, called Elite Trucking in Canoga Park. The company looks solid. Legitimate. And I don't have any reason to believe otherwise."

"But you'd like me to take a closer look," Louis said, as I turned on to Owensmouth and drove north.

"Exactly. And look good and close at the head of the company, name of Irving Sherman."

"Why are this company and guy of interest to you?"

"I'm investigating the death – about a year ago — of a resident of one of those assisted living and retirement homes. A man named Abe Levy. The manner of death was ruled to be natural, and the cause as heart failure. But I'm finding things that are getting me to think the man was killed."

"There are two connections between Levy and Sherman, that you should be aware of. The first is that they're both survivors of the World War II concentration camp, Auschwitz."

"According to Levy's granddaughter, Levy and Sherman may

have done some nasty things in Auschwitz—and the theory I'm looking at, is that Sherman may have arranged Levy's death, because he was afraid that some details about what they did there, might come out."

"Why now? So many years later? Because Levy was sinking into dementia, and talking more and more about what they did in the camp."

"And the second connection, is that Sherman and Levy both worked at Elite, and then, as partners, they bought the company, after the owner died. Then, a few years later, Sherman bought Levy out, but I don't know why."

Louis asked, "You want me to ask about Sherman and Elite, up and down, in and out. Plus a check of Levy and his connection with Elite. Do I have that right?"

"That's what I want."

"Going to cost you, Will."

"How much?"

"A thousand to start. Maybe more. Not sure."

"Your rates have gone up."

"There's inflation working all the time, Will."

"Hey, Louis, the Federal Reserve says inflation is under control."

"Maybe in DC. But not in my business environs."

Dear Reader –did you note Louis and his discussion about inflation, the Federal Reserve and such words as 'business environs'? That is pure Louis The Fisherman. Smart, and a businessman. Go figure. A snitch like no other.

"Okay. The terms are fine," I told Louis. "Any idea how long?"

"When I know, you'll know."

Louis looked over his shoulder.

I assured him, "Your trail car is there."

I'd spotted the car right after we turned on to Owensmouth.

Louis smiled at me. "Hey, Will, you still think like a cop. Good for you."

He nodded curbside. "Pull up here."

I did, and Louis got out.

"Go!" he ordered.

And I did that, too.

Looking in my rear view mirror, I saw Louis get into the other car, which turned right at the next corner.

Goodbye, Louis.

CHAPTER ELEVEN

After my meeting with Louis, I headed home, to Tarzana, about a twenty minute ride from where I was, in Canoga Park.

When I opened the front door, I was ready to try Lu's latest cooking adventure, but no savory smells came my way.

Instead, Lu was standing in the hallway, wrapped in a towel, her hair still wet from what I figured was a shower – hey, I'm a detective -- I can detect, and deduce.

And as per usual, she was holding my evening cocktail – club soda on the rocks. I took the glass, gave Lu a grateful kiss, and asked, "So, what're you cooking tonight? How come nothing smells wonderful?"

"Because you're taking me out to dinner," Lu answered. "You owe me, big time."

"Why is that?"

Lu held up the file folder that was in her other hand.

"Because I've got your report. All you ever wanted to know about those gentlemen – Semanksi, Fedorov, Beletski and Levenbuk."

"You found them?"

"Not only did I find them. I've given you mucho detail on each. From when they arrived in the U.S., right up to the present time."

She tapped the file with her free hand.

"This was me at my best. Researching – and yes – hacking – immigration records, court records, social security files, you name it –I searched and I hacked."

Lu handed me the file.

"Why don't you go read, while I finish getting dressed?" she suggested.

So I did, and she did.

Taking them one at a time, here's what Lu found.

First, Semanski. This is the one I already knew, from what Ally Morris had told me. Yes, Lu's search confirmed what Ally had said — that Semanski was Irving Sherman. He had entered the U.S. in 1946, and after the mandatory five years of permanent residency, he became a citizen in 1951. Later that year, he changed his name from Isadore Semanski to Irving Sherman. Earlier, in 1950, he had gone to work at Elite Trucking, where he was now president.

Next, there's the other one I already knew — Ally's grandfather – current name of Abraham Levy. According to Lu's report, he also got to the U.S. in 1946, and similar to Semanski, he became a citizen in 1951. In that year, too, he changed his name from Abraham Levenbuk to Levy, but he kept his first name, Abraham. Levy went to work at Elite Trucking in 1951, and I guessed that Sherman brought him in there.

Third on the list I had given Lu was someone named Fedorov. This person, Lu was able to track as one Isaac Fedorov. Came to the U.S. in 1946, became a citizen in 1951, and changed his name to Elliott Freid. And – no surprise – he, too, went to work at Elite in 1951. And again, I figured that Sherman brought him in.

And finally, there was Beletski, first name...Binyamin. Yup. Same pattern. Entered the U.S. in 1946, a citizen in 1951, changed his name to Ben Binder, joined Elite in 1951.

I already knew that Levy was dead, and that Sherman was still alive and the president of Elite, but I wondered what the current status was, of Freid and Binder. Lu had information on this, too. Clearly, dinner was going to cost me!

Freid had retired from Elite in 1995. He was 65 at the time, and that's when he started drawing his social security checks. Now 73, he was still alive, and getting those checks, at an address in the San Fernando Valley.

Binder had retired from Elite in 1990, also at the age of 65. He was now 78, and also getting his social security checks at an address in the San Fernando Valley.

My mind went skipping over several thoughts.

I thought about the fact that these four guys had been together ever since Auschwitz – that goes back to 1942 – a full 61 years ago. And their shared experiences at the camp. And their parallel lives in all the years since. And their vows of silence about what they did in the camp – at least according to what Ally Morris said her grandfather told her grandmother.

And I thought about the three visitors who came to see Levy in those last four months before he died – the people who signed in as Smith, Jones and West. And I wondered – no, I suspected, that they might really be Silver, Freid and Binder – checking to see if Grandpa Levy was talking too much about what they did in Auschwitz, as he sank deeper into his dementia.

I decided I needed to see that attendant again – Edwin Nesbitt. I wanted to question him about any visitors Abe Levy had. Nesbit said he never heard any names from Levy, but maybe if I mentioned Semanski, Fedorov and Beletsky– as well as their Americanized versions -- it might jar loose some memories on Nesbitt's part. Sure worth a try.

CHAPTER TWELVE

The next day, I had Rose call Vistas and find out when Nesbitt would be on duty. What I wanted to do was to catch him at the end of his shift. Surprise him. And hit him with the names. And I had some other questions for him, too.

Nesbitt, Rose found out, was working 8AM to 4PM – so I arrived at Vistas by 3:45. I drove to the section of the parking area marked: Staff Parking Only, and waited. A few minutes after 4, Nesbitt came out of Vistas and walked toward a two door Mercedes, an E300 model, in red, with chrome wheels. Very neat looking. And with a price tag, I figured, well into the $40K+ range.

Right away, my suspicious mind latched on to the idea that this was a lot of car for a nursing home attendant to be driving. Takes money to buy it, pay for the insurance, the registration, the upkeep.

And of course, my next suspicious thought had to be – where'd Nesbitt get this kind of money? Something I needed to ask him about.

"Mr. Nesbitt," I said, approaching him as he neared his car. "Can we talk, please?"

Nesbitt stopped, turned, and saw me.

Did I imagine he got a bit uptight?

"Will Jonas," I said. "We met a few days ago."

Nesbitt nodded.

"What do you want?"

On purpose, I came closer, crowded him, almost forced him to lean back up against his car. I was hoping that my height advantage would make him a bit uncomfortable -- my six feet four inches over his –I'm guessing – five feet 10 inches. It worked. Nesbitt looked a bit edgy.

"I want to check with you, about possible visitors that Abe Levy had."

"I already told you everything I remembered," Nesbitt said.

"Yes, I know. But here's the thing. One of the people living in Vistas does recall Mr. Levy mentioning a few names, so I wanted to mention them to you, too. Maybe it'll jar your memory."

I smiled, all friendly.

"All right?"

Nesbitt didn't say anything, so I pressed.

"All right, if I ask you?"

I stared down at him and he nodded.

"Okay, here goes. Did Levy ever mention these names?"

"Semanski?"

I waited for an answer.

"No."

"Fedorov?"

"No."

"Or Beletski?"

"No."

"You sure?" I pressed on purpose.

"Yes, I'm sure."

Nesbitt definitely was uncomfortable now. I continued.

"Okay, here are three more names for you."

"Silver?"

"No."

"Freid?"

"No."

"Binder?"

"No."

I stared at Nesbitt. Didn't say anything for a few seconds. Then I continued.

"You know, I don't understand. I really don't. Do you know what I don't understand?" I challenged him.

"No...I don't."

Nesbitt made a move toward his car, but I blocked his way, and continued talking.

"What I don't understand is how you never heard any of those names –while someone else who knew Levy, heard him mention some of those names, several times, in the months before he died. How can that be?" I asked.

Now, Nesbitt was clearly upset — and it seemed to me — frightened.

"I don't know anything!" he said. "I don't know what you're talking about. I want to go now!"

I leaned my arm up against the car door, keeping Nesbitt from opening it.

"Did you know that Dr. Clayton was killed about six months ago?" I asked.

This shook Nesbitt up.

"I...I knew. Yes, I heard about it."

"A hit and run accident. At least, that's what it looked like."

"What...what do you mean?" Nesbitt asked. "What do you mean — that's what it looked like?"

"What I mean is...I'm thinking it may not have been an accident at all. Killing Dr. Clayton may have been a deliberate act of murder."

When I said this, I saw it in his face! Damn it! I saw real fear in Nesbitt's face. I was on to something here.

"I'm still trying to figure out *why* Clayton may have been killed. You wouldn't know anything about that, would you?"

"Of course not!" Nesbitt said, his voice up tight, shrill.

He tried again, to reach for his car door, but I kept my arm leveraged against it. Then I made a show of looking closely at his car.

"Good looking set of wheels you're driving, Nesbitt. Looks new. When did you get it?"

"A few month ago."

"Must have cost in the high $40's. Didn't know your job paid that well. What'd it cost?"

"If you want to know, go buy one," he challenged me.

Nesbitt seemed to get some of his confidence back. And I could see that I'd probably not get anything more out of him. Time to let it go – at least for now.

"Nice talking with you," I said. "But I have a feeling we'll have another go-round very soon," I added.

"I don't think so," Nesbitt shot back. "Stay away from me, Jonas, or I'll make a complaint to the police. You're not a cop. I don't have to talk to you."

CHAPTER THIRTEEN

Despite my show of confidence with Nesbitt, I was up against a blank wall, when it came to my trying to establish that Sherman, Freid and Binder had visited Abe Levy in those last four months, when Smith, Jones and West were the names showing up on the visitors' register at Vistas.

Yes, I did have Polly Gladstein telling me that Levy did mention Semanski, Freid and Beletski in his dementia-related comments. And yes, I did know that these Polish names had been changed by their owners into their Americanized versions – Sherman, Freid and Binder.

But so what? This still did not directly establish that one or more of those guys was visiting Levy in those last four months before he died. And *that* was the link – the connection – I was missing.

So, how to find that link?

I thought about this, on my drive back to my office, after seeing Nesbitt, and by the time I got there, I had figured out a possible way to do it.

How, you ask?

Here's how.

Polly Gladstein had told me she heard Abe Levy mention those three original Polish names—Semanski, Fedorov and Beletski.

Okay, what I was now going to bet is that Polly – let's face it – was one of those folks who likes to know what everyone around her, is doing. And if I'm right about this, then I'm betting that Polly probably saw any and all visitors that Abe Levy had. She hadn't said so to me. But I bet she was the type who liked to see who visited who in Vistas.

In my office, I spoke with Rose, told her what I was thinking – and first off, I learned a new word – a Yiddish word that Rose taught me. It was – "yenta." And what did it mean? Here's how Rose explained it.

"A yenta," she told me, "is someone who needs to know everything about everyone, and who then enjoys talking about what she knows. Your Polly sounds like a typical yenta."

I thought for a moment, and then asked, "Do you think you might be able to find pictures of Sherman, Freid and Binder?"

"Sherman is easy. He's president of Elite. I'm sure there are pictures in some paper, or somewhere."

She thought for a moment.

"About Freid and Binder – if...if they are still driving, then there are the pictures on their drivers' licenses."

"You can get those?" I asked. "How do you get those?"

Stupid question, I realized. My wife, Lu, was a whiz at using a computer to retrieve information – public or otherwise. Rose was almost as good.

"You don't worry about the details," Rose said. "You'll have the pictures by later today, or tomorrow morning."

"Good. And I want two more pictures. One of them is for that attendant at Vistas – Edwin Nesbitt. And the other is for that doctor, who died about six months ago in that hit and run. Dr. Amos Clayton."

"Nesbitt is no problem," Rose said. "Dr. Clayton may be a little harder."

"Well, if you're having a problem with Clayton, let me know. I can always ask his wife for a picture—although I'd rather not. She's a nice lady, and I don't especially want to disturb her with another discussion about her husband's death."

"Okay."

"One more thing I need you to look up," I said. "On Nesbitt, see if you can find out when he bought a new car. It's a Mercedes 300E. I'd like to know where he got it, the terms, with his trade-in, the net price – all that sort of stuff. Can do?"

"Of course," answered my resident hacker.

"Ah, ain't this computer age just wonderful."

Rose looked at her notes and sighed.

"All this, because someone couldn't leave that poor old man – a concentration camp survivor – die in his own time. Someone had to kill him, for some reason."

Rose shook her head.

"As I said before, I can forgive anything that anyone did in those concentration camps. When you want to survive those horrors – well – I won't judge anyone's actions."

She shook her head again.

"But to kill a concentration camp survivor? After all the years of suffering that person went through…to kill someone like that…it is wrong. It is so wrong."

"I agree," I said.

I stepped behind my desk, took off my holster and my Glock 19, and put them in their usual place, the top right drawer.

"Going to see Charlie," I told Rose. "Sure don't need my piece for that meeting."

"Did you put the safety on?" Rose teased me.

I laughed.

"Ever since I gave you that gun lecture, you just love to check up on me, don't you?"

"Well," Rose said. "You're not getting any younger. You might forget. I just want to make sure."

I decided to leave the office. No way was I going to win this back and forth with Rose. As a matter of fact, I rarely do. Now *that's* a fact I wouldn't mind forgetting.

CHAPTER FOURTEEN

"A very satisfying sandwich," Charlie said, finishing off his pastrami-on-rye, followed by a forkful of potato salad.

We were eating at Brent's in Northridge– one of the best delicatessens in the Greater Los Angeles area.

"With you, Charlie," I said, "Every sandwich is satisfying."

"Well, good food means good living. And good living is what it's all about."

"In your case, what good food means is that I'm looking at your stomach, but I can't see your belt buckle. It's covered by a layer of you-know-what."

"You're just jealous, Will. Because you don't eat like me. Don't enjoy food like I do."

Charlie patted his stomach.

"True, there's a bit more here, than used to be. But I am having a good time growing it."

Charlie, even when he was 10-15 years younger, and my partner, was always on the less-than-lean side. He stands five nine, and weighs about195 pounds. But what he lacks in buff, Charlie more than makes up, with what's between his ears. He is one of the smartest people I know.

"Okay, Will, I need a fill-in," Charlie said. "See if it's time to bring this investigation inside – before Klinger hears about it, and goes ballistic on me."

"Not there yet, Charlie. Making progress, though."

I brought Charlie up to date on my efforts to tie Sherman, Freid and Binder – to the visits to Abe Levy, and about Nesbitt being able to buy a $40K+ new Mercedes.

"All good, but still lots of air," Charlie pointed out.

"Yeah, I know. But I'm planning on seeing Polly Gladstein again, as soon as I have pictures of Sherman, Freid and Binder. I'm hoping she can ID them as being visitors to Levy. *Then* I'd have something solid. Something I can confront the three of them with. Try to dig and find out why they were visiting Levy so frequently in those last four months. And how come they used phony names for the visits."

"That'd be good," Charlie agreed.

"And on Nesbitt, I've asked Rose to find out when he bought that new Mercedes. Who knows? If my theory is right – that Dr. Clayton was paid off – then that's got to mean that Nesbitt also was paid off. Both of them. And there we'd have it, Charlie — Levy being murdered, just like he and his wife and his granddaughter were worried about."

Charlie took another forkful of potato salad.

"Sounds good, Will, but like we both know, it's all circumstantial. We have nothing specific, that ties Nesbitt and Clayton to killing Levy. And on the payoffs, how do you track those back to Sherman, Freid and Binder? To them being the ones who paid Nesbitt and Clayton?"

"That'll come, Charlie. That'll come."

"Okay, I can go with that, for right now."

Charlie took a file folder that was next to him, and handed it to me.

"The details on Clayton's hit and run death. It's all in there."

"Thanks."

Charlie looked at the glass display case at the far end of the restaurant.

"No, Charlie," I told him. "You cannot have any cheesecake."

CHAPTER FIFTEEN

Rose, bless her hacking heart, gave me pictures of Sherman, Freid and Binder, when I arrived at the office the following day.

Armed with the shots, I drove over to Vistas, to see Polly Gladstein. When I got there, I caught a good break. Polly was seated in the same chair on the porch, as when she had called out to me, that previous time we'd talked. The chair was near the front door, and I couldn't help thinking—that's an ideal spot for keeping an eye on things. Polly being a yenta, is what Rose would call it, right?

Polly spotted me when I got out of my car. She waved, and I waved back. I walked toward the front entrance, then went left on the porch and joined Polly at her outpost.

"Good to see you again, Polly," I said, sitting down.

"Good to see you, Will."

Polly smiled dramatically and batted her eyelashes.

"We meet again. Tell me, what are your intentions?"

"Honorable," I said.

"That's what I was afraid you would say." Polly smiled, this time, a real smile. "So, why *are* you here?"

"To see if you can help me with something."

"And that would be?"

"Remember those three names you gave me? The Polish names that Abe Levy kept mentioning?"

"Semanski, Fedorov and Beletski," Polly fed back to me.

"Right. Well, we've tracked those names – and we've been able to establish that all three of them came to the U.S. after World War Two. And that they all changed their names. Semanski became Sherman, Fedorov turned into Freid, and Beletski ended up as Binder."

"We also suspect that all three of these men may have visited Abe Levy, here at Vistas, especially in the four or so months before Mr. Levy died."

I held up the file folder I had with me.

"I've got pictures of all three men."

"And you want me to see if I recognize any of them?"

"Right," I said. "I'm going to show them to you, one a time. Okay?"

"Okay."

I took out the first picture – the shot of Sherman/Semanski – and put it on the table, in front of Polly.

Polly put on her glasses, looked at the picture, and nodded.

"Yes. He came to see Abe. More than once."

"You're sure?"

"I'm sure."

I took out the photo of Binder/Beletski.

"What about this one?"

Polly looked.

"Yes. He came, too. More than once."

"And this one," I asked, putting the shot of Freid/Fedorov on the table.

"Him, too. He also came more than once."

Polly was no dummy. She stared across at me.

"So, what is this all about, Mr. Private Investigator? Why all this interest in Abe Levy and who came to see him?"

I shook my head.

"I'm sorry. Right now, I can't answer that question, Polly."

For emphasis, I leaned across the table and looked closely at her.

"But I can tell you, that what I'm doing is important. And what's also important, is that you don't ask me any more questions, right now. Or, talk to anyone else about what we've been discussing. Can you promise me that, Polly? In return, I will make you this promise. When the timing is right, I will tell you everything. I will answer all of your questions. Okay? Do I have your promise?"

Polly looked at me, and it was clear she understood that this was a serious matter.

"All right," she said. "I do promise."

CHAPTER SIXTEEN

Rose had also managed to get pictures of Edwin Nesbitt and Dr. Amos Clayton, so I decided it was time that night to hit the two bars where Clayton usually did his drinking.

What was I looking for? Answers to questions about Clayton's hit and run death. For one thing, it was bugging me, that Clayton was run over, in the back alley of a Chatsworth bar, 15 miles away from the bars his wife said he usually went to.

Why was Clayton in Chatsworth? He had no way of getting there. No car. It had been repossessed.

The obvious answer? Someone drove him there.

And I was thinking, that someone could well have been Nesbitt. Here's my reasoning.

As I'd already suggested to Charlie, if Abe Levy was murdered, then Nesbitt and Clayton were the ones involved. Nesbitt doing the dirty deed. Then Clayton signing the death certificate claiming it was a natural causes death due to heart failure.

Then – just after he gets a second, five thousand dollars – Clayton is run over and killed. That looks to me like whoever was paying him off, decided enough was enough. He may have figured that Clayton either would come back for even more money. Or that the doctor might babble all the wrong things in one of his drunken states. So, he had to kill him. Or more likely, he ordered Nesbitt to kill Clayton.

What I hoped to find out, when visiting Clayton's favorite bars, was whether anyone saw him there, drinking, on the night he was killed. And – if Nesbitt – or anyone else — was with him.

I called Mrs. Clayton and she gave me the names of the two bars. They were a couple of blocks apart, on Vanowen, just west of the Clayton apartment on Odessa, in Van Nuys.

The first bar was named – believe it, I don't make these things up – The Jolly Roger. And as you might have expected, it was anything but Jolly, when I came in, about 7:30.

Two solo drinkers were anchored to the bar, looking like they had been there for several hours. And two couples were at tables on opposite ends of the room. They also looked like they had permanent occupancy rights.

But the main man I was interested in, was the bartender. He was in his late thirties or early forties, with an open and friendly face, a greeter of all patrons. A name plate over his left, breast pocket let me know his was "Joe."

"Welcome to the Jolly Roger," Joe said, as I sat down at the bar. "What's your pleasure?"

"A tall club soda," I said. "I'm a recovering alcoholic. Been so, for seven years, and aim to keep it that way."

Joe smiled, extended his hand and we shook.

"Good for you," he said, clearly meaning it. "So what brings you in here?"

I took Clayton's picture out of the envelope I was carrying, and laid it on the bar.

"Do you recognize this person?" I asked. "His wife told me he used to come in here, regularly."

Joe looked at the picture and nodded.

"And suppose I do? Why is it you want to know? What am I dealing with here?"

Couldn't blame the guy for being cautious. So, I gave him a few details. Not anyway accurate, of course, but it served the purpose.

"His name is Amos Clayton. Doctor Amos Clayton."

Joe nodded. "Okay. I agree. Yes, I do know him."

"I'm a private investigator – working for the insurance company that's wrapping up its file on Clayton's being killed by a hit and run driver."

Joe was surprised.

"Doc is dead? A hit and run accident? *That* I didn't know. Yeah, he hasn't been in for a long time, now that I think of it –but I figured he was just back on the wagon again. That was his pattern. On then off. On then off."

"Okay, here's the thing," I said. "The accident happened in the alley behind a bar up in Chatsworth. And we're trying to figure out why Clayton was drinking, way out there. His wife told me that, as far as she knew, her husband did his drinking here – and at Whiskey Plus – up the street."

"She's right," Joe confirmed. "I know Whiskey Plus. And I'm pretty sure our two bars are where Doc did his drinking. And what's more, when he'd come close to passing out, we both had his home telephone number. We'd call Mrs. Clayton, and she'd come and take him home."

Joe shook his head.

"She's a nice lady, I can tell you. She deserved better. But she always stood by Doc. She'd come, when we called. She never yelled at him, or said anything bad to him. She'd just settle up his bill and take him away."

I said, "Well, on the night he was run over in Chatsworth, we're pretty certain that someone – not his wife — came here – or to Whiskey Plus – and took Clayton up there."

I took out Nesbitt's photo from the envelope and showed it to Joe.

"This guy look familiar?" I asked. "Did you see him in here? And maybe take Clayton out with him?"

Joe studied the picture.

"No. He doesn't look familiar. I don't think I've ever seen him. Here or anywhere."

"You're sure?"

Joe nodded.

"I'm good at remembering faces. It comes with the territory. And this is not a face I remember."

He thought for a second.

"Have you been to Whiskey Plus, yet?"

"No. You were the first stop."

"I'll tell you what. Let me call Mike – he runs the bar over there – and I'll tell him you're coming over – and why. He'll cooperate with you. He'll want to help. Just like I do. Because Mrs. Clayton deserves a break."

A little while later, at Whiskey Plus, Mike did recognize Nesbitt.

"Yeah. He was in here, sitting with Doc Clayton. Can't be sure, when. But six or so months ago, seems about right."

"You're sure?"

"One hundred per cent? No. Eighty per cent? Yes."

Mike went and filled an order at the other end of the bar. When he came back, he explained what he meant.

"One of the reasons I remember the guy with Doc, was that he

59

wasn't drinking. Not like you, though. Not AA. He did order something. And I did see him take a sip every once in a while. But the thing is, he nursed it. Just the one drink, I'm pretty sure. While Clayton kept drinking steadily. And I think – I can't be absolutely sure – but I think this guy paid the tab. Clayton didn't. He was pretty smashed when they left. I remember thinking, it was nice that someone else, besides Mrs. Clayton, was going to take Doc home. He had just about passed out, at that point."

Progress, huh?

Thanks to Joe and Mike, I could now tie Nesbitt and Clayton together on the night that Clayton was run over.

Okay, let's keep building the case I told myself. On to Chatsworth.

From Whiskey Plus on Vanowen, I drove west, to Mason, turned right and took Mason, north to Devonshire. Then west on Devonshire for one block, and I arrived at El Amigo. Parking was in the rear, so that's where I went.

There was a large sized parking lot, about three quarters full. Much more active place than the two neighborhood bars I'd just come from. There also was an alley that ran east to west, shared by the backside of El Amigo, plus the rear of the several other buildings in the immediate block.

According to the accident report Charlie had given me, Clayton was run over in that alley. I parked my car and walked along the alley. In the area immediately between El Amigo and its parking lot, the alley was well lit.

But once you got beyond El Amigo, the alley was dark. And according to the accident report, it was in that darker part of the alley that Clayton was run over, killed, and the driver ran.

The report said that it appeared that Clayton was lying in the alley, when the hit and run car, ran right over him.

What the hell was he doing, lying in the middle of the alley? Had he passed out, from too much alcohol? Or was he somehow pushed, so he fell down in front of the oncoming car?

No way of telling. Just another of the unsolved hit and runs that occurred every year in Los Angeles, or for that matter, in any major city.

What I did know was this.

That Nesbitt was feeding Clayton drinks on the night the doctor died.

That Nesbitt walked the very drunk Clayton out of Whiskey Plus that same night.

That Nesbitt had a new car. Maybe the old one was damaged if it was involved in the hit and run? Damage that Nesbitt would want to cover up and not report?

Okay, so now it was time to see if I could place Nesbitt and Clayton in El Amigo, before Clayton was run over. I went back to my car, left the Clayton accident file, picked up the envelope containing the Nesbitt and Clayton pictures, and walked across the parking lot to the back entrance.

The scene inside El Amigo was all-the-way-different from the two earlier bars I'd visited. This bar was busy. Most of the counter stools and all of the tables in the bar area were occupied. And at the far end of the room, I saw an entry way into a restaurant.

I walked up to the bar and nodded at the nearest bartender – there were three of them working. The one I had nodded to, came over, and I pushed a folded twenty across to him.

I asked, "Can I buy a couple of minutes of your time, please?"

He pocketed the twenty and smiled.

"Your money. Your minutes. What can I do for you?"

"Jerry" – that's what his name tag said, "I want to see if you can recognize a couple of people who may have been in here – about six months ago – when that man was killed out back, in that hit and run."

Jerry grinned.

"You could have saved the twenty, Mister. I told the cops everything I knew – which was just about nothing. They interviewed me – interviewed all of us – the night that it happened."

"Yes, I read the report."

I took out Clayton's picture and laid it on the counter.

"So, did the cops show you a picture of the victim? His name's Amos Clayton."

Jerry looked and nodded.

"Yup. They showed me a picture the next day. I think it was probably a morgue shot. You know. Eyes closed. He looked dead."

Jerry tapped Clayton's picture.

"That's the same guy. In his better days, I guess."

"And did the police ask you if Clayton had been in here?"

"Yes, they did. And I told them that he had. He was pretty soused when he came in. And he had a couple of drinks here. Then, he was at the point where I wasn't going to serve him anymore. And I told him so."

"Tell me, was Clayton with anyone?"

Jerry nodded.

"Yes. There was someone with him. He was sober. And when I told Clayton I wouldn't serve him anymore, his friend said he'd take care of him. And he steered him out of here. Clayton was just about totally out of it. The other man, he was sober."

"According to the police report," I said, "You couldn't tell them much about the person with Clayton. Couldn't give much of a description."

Jerry shrugged.

"Like every night, it was busy. I remembered Clayton, because he was so soused, and not one of our regulars. The other guy? I just remembered him, kind of generally. He definitely wasn't one of our regulars, though."

I took Nesbitt's picture out of the envelope and put it on the bar.

"This person look familiar to you?" I asked.

Jerry looked at the picture. For a long time.

"Well, I think this. I think I do recognize him. As the person with Clayton. But if I had to swear to it, I couldn't. He looks familiar, but – you know – kind of fuzzily so. You get what I'm saying? I'd give pretty good odds that he was with Clayton. But it definitely was not a sure thing."

I nodded at the other two bartenders.

"Possible that one of them would recognize this picture?"

Jerry shook his head.

"You can ask them, of course. But Clayton was sitting at this end of the bar, along with the other guy – and this is the end of the bar that I take care of. Neither of the other bartenders would have served them."

CHAPTER SEVENTEEN

By the time I got home after my barhopping, Lu was asleep. And the next morning, I was still sleeping, when she left for work. So it wasn't until that evening that I had a chance to see my beautiful wife.

We were eating dinner, when I told Lu, "I've decided to give you a new name."

"And what would that be?"

"The Gourmet Chef of Tarzana – and maybe even of the whole San Fernando Valley."

Tonight, working her way through her recently acquired cookbook, Lu had made Veal Parmigiana with thin spaghetti, topped with a marina sauce. At least, that's what she told me I'd eaten. I didn't know much about the dishes Lu was preparing, in her new hobby of cooking. My job was to do the eating. It was up to Lu to label the dishes for me.

"I thank you for the title," Lu said. "But I'm not done yet. The title I'm going for is, 'Gourmet Chef of Los Angeles.'"

"And I'll be happy to eat my way, in pursuit of that title," I told her. "After all, what's a husband for – if not to support his wife in her ambitions?"

"So," Lu said, changing topics, "Three bars in one night, and club soda in all? That's impressive."

"Yeah. Wasn't that hard. Just a little nudge that didn't really bother me."

"How's the case coming along?" Lu asked. "Any closer to determining if that man's death was natural? Or murder?"

"A lot closer. In fact, I'm sure he was murdered. Trouble is, most of what I have is circumstantial. It makes sense. But no hard facts to back things up."

"So what's next?"

"It's time to see the three guys who were close to Abe Levy. The ones he told his wife he was afraid might kill him, because of what he knew. I want to confront each of them. Tell them what I have, and let's see how they react."

"When do you start?"

"Tomorrow. I've got addresses on all three. One of them is

running Elite Trucking, so I know where to reach him. But I want to save him for last. I think he's probably the top dog among them. The other two are retired. May be a little easier to deal with. To confront."

CHAPTER EIGHTEEN

What'd someone once say about "the best laid plans..."? I forget the rest of it, but the meaning's clear – whatever you plan, it ain't necessarily going to happen that way.

Prime example? I'd told Lu that I planned to see the late Abe Levy's three friends, but in a particular order. That is, Binder, then Freid, then Sherman – the last one being the top dog.

But when I arrived in my office the next morning, Rose was already in, and she greeted me with the following.

"A man named Irving Sherman of Elite Trucking called. Sounded mad. Said you would know who he is. Said he wanted to see you – to quote his exact words – 'Damn soon this morning. Tell him to come to my office. I'll be expecting him.'"

"He sounded mad, huh? Did he say what he was angry about?"

"I didn't have a chance to ask him anything," Rose said. "I answered the phone...he asked for you...I said you weren't in...he said what I told you he said...and he hung up."

"Call Sherman back, and tell him I'm on my way," I told Rose.

Elite Trucking was on Canoga Avenue in Canoga Park, just north of Roscoe Boulevard. From my office in Woodland Hills, it was about five miles away – a ten-minute trip.

Driving over, I used the time to think about how I wanted to handle the meeting. Judging by the message he'd left with Rose, I figured Sherman had heard some of what I'd been doing. Probably from Nesbitt. Couldn't make him happy. I was sure he'd want to know what else I was up to. And I had a bunch of questions for him. Going to be an interesting meeting, Folks. Stay around for it.

Elite Trucking occupied a fair sized plot of land on the west side of Canoga Avenue. The main building was a single story, stretching horizontally about 50 yards, with a front entrance located about mid-point.

There was a large parking area to the right of the building, with several trucks on it, a mix of small vans and bigger trucks – all with the Elite Trucking logo on their sides. Part of the Elite delivery fleet, I assumed.

I went in the front entrance of the main building, and a receptionist greeted me.

"Mr. Jonas? Mr. Sherman is expecting you." She nodded to my left. "Please go down that hall and Mr. Sherman will meet you."

I started down the short hall and saw a tall, beefy guy come out of an office at the end, and stand there. Shirt sleeves rolled up to his elbows, a tie pulled down, and the top button of his shirt unbuttoned.

"Jonas?" he growled, "In here."

Sherman turned and went back into his office. I followed.

When he reached his desk, Sherman didn't sit down. Instead, he turned and glowered – yep, glowered is the operative word – at me.

"What the hell are you doing, going around Vistas, asking questions about Abe Levy's death a year ago?"

Good, I thought to myself, this confirms that he's got an informant at Vistas. Was it Nesbitt, the attendant, I wondered?

"How'd you know I was asking questions about Mr. Levy's death?" I countered.

"Not important," he snapped. "What is important is – *why* are you asking questions?"

I told him, "Because Abe Levy's granddaughter asked me to. She doesn't think her grandfather died a natural death."

Sherman was jolted. He tried to hide it, and almost did. But my answer did bother him.

"She doesn't know what she's talking about," he came back at me. "The death certificate said Abe died of natural causes. That's what the doctor wrote."

"How come you know so much about Levy's death?" I asked. "You're not part of the family."

"I'm damn close to it," he said. "Abe and I go back a long way. To Auschwitz during World War Two. And then we were partners here in Elite. So when Abe got sick, started going downhill, I kept tabs on him."

I decided to hit him with another hard one.

"Is that why you, and Binder and Freid went to Vistas – those last four months that Levy was alive — and signed the visitors register as Smith, Jones and West?"

Again, Sherman was jolted. And again, he got aggressive in trying to cover it up.

"What the hell are you saying? You got no way of backing that up!"

"The hell I don't! I have an eye witness who's identified all three of you as having visited Levy at Vistas."

And then I stretched the truth a bit by adding, "On those very days that you guys were signing in as Smith, Jones and West."

A few seconds passed. I watched as Sherman took some deep breaths, obviously reviewing his strategy on how he wanted to deal with me. When he spoke again, it was in a less aggressive tone.

"Look, here's the deal. All four of us have been close, for 60 years, starting in Auschwitz, and then afterwards, right up to now. When Abe got sick, when the dementia started getting serious, when he went into Vistas, we were concerned for him. But when I bought Abe out from our partnership in Elite, it was...well...it wasn't a nice deal. He and I both walked away from that, with some bitter tastes in our mouths. And Binder and Freid, too. They weren't partners, but they were working here."

"So we had two things going here. We wanted to visit Abe. But we didn't want his family to know we were doing it. So, we decided we'd each sign in with a false name."

Sherman shrugged and held his hands out, palms up.

"Seems kind of stupid now. But that's why we did it."

I didn't believe a word of what he'd said, but I decided not to let him know. Just let him hang on that, I figured. And I then hit him with another question.

I told Sherman, "I know that Levy was regretting some of the things the four of you did in Auschwitz – to survive. I'm told – that as his dementia was getting worse and worse, he started talking about – 'the killing...the killing.' What's that all about?"

Sherman shrugged.

"Yeah, I know about that. But that was just his dementia talking. There was no truth to what Abe was saying at that point."

Sherman shook his head.

"Look, Jonas...we did a lot of things in the camp, to survive –

but we never killed anyone in Auschwitz. Never! This was all in Abe's imagination. In his dementia. That's all that it was."

Sherman turned and waved at one of the walls in his office. It was his "brag wall" – the wall that had all of the pictures of him with various local public figures, and awards he'd received. I'd seen heavier walls, but Sherman's was pretty impressive.

He said to me, in a less confrontational tone, "Ever since I got to this country, I've tried to be a good and responsible citizen. It's paid off. I've got this company." He waved again at the wall. "And I've done my share of good things. I've worked hard to get where I am. I'm proud of my reputation. And I am not happy with what you are doing. I'm not happy at all!"

Time to make him even more unhappy, I decided.

"Yeah," I said, "I see the good things you've done. But there are other things that are bothering me."

"Like what?"

"Like the fact that the doctor who signed off on Levy's death certificate, received two, five thousand dollar payments. One right after Levy died. Then a second one about six months ago. Right after which, he was killed in a hit and run. Lots of suspicious stuff there, that I need to investigate."

"And how about the attendant who was responsible for Abe Levy – Edwin Nesbitt? He got himself a forty thousand dollar Mercedes. No way, he could afford that car on what he made at Vistas. So that's something I need to look into."

With my comments about Clayton and Nesbitt, I'd purposely baited Sherman. I wanted him to know how deeply I had dug, in my investigation. And that I planned to keep digging. I wanted to see what his reaction would be.

And what was it?

Alpha Time.

Sherman took a deep breath and stood as tall as he could. He was just about the same height as me.

"Don't fuck with me and my reputation, Jonas. You'll be sorry. I promise you that. Now, get the hell out of my company!"

So I left.

CHAPTER NINETEEN

On the way out of the Elite building, I again noticed the company trucks parked on the lot, and a thought hit me.

Amos Clayton was killed in a hit and run. I'm thinking that Edwin Nesbitt was the driver. So, I'm wondering if maybe he'd used one of the smaller Elite delivery vans, for that purpose. If he was working for Sherman and the others, well, why not? Certainly, something to consider.

But before I went off on that angle, I realized that what I had to do next, was to see the two other members of the original friends group – Elliott Freid and Ben Binder. And the sooner I could get to those guys, the better. Now that I had seen Sherman, I was sure he'd talk to both of them, about his meeting with me. To discuss how to keep their answers in line with what he'd told me.

Rose had given me Freid's and Binder's home addresses – they both were retired – and I was hoping they'd be at home. I looked at my notes to see who was closest to where I now was. It was Binder. His address was 7315 Leadwell Street in Winnetka, a couple of blocks south of Saticoy.

To get there, I drove south on Canoga, then east on Roscoe to Winnetka, right on Winnetka to Leadwell, right again, and then half way down the block, there it was, on my right, a large condo complex, called Georgian Arms.

Georgian Arms, I asked myself? Odd name. Why'd the developer pick it? Damned if I knew, but it wasn't a mystery I felt I needed to solve.

I was hoping to see Binder, unannounced. Catch him by surprise. Not give him any time to plan and rehearse his answers – even if Sherman had managed to call him, before I got there.

I parked and walked up to the complex's locked entry gate, where I caught some good luck. A woman was coming out. So, I put on my sincerest smile, and nodded my thanks to her, as I walked in, through the gate she had opened. Then, in case she was watching, I started walking down the path inside, as if I knew where I was going. Could have saved myself the trouble. When I looked back, the lady had walked away. So much for gated security, huh?

Binder lived in unit 21. I checked the number on the nearest unit, and continued down the path, and then down another path to my right, until I came to 21.

I walked up to the front door, rang the bell and waited. Nothing.

I gave it a few more seconds, then pushed the bell again.

"All right, I'm coming," I heard.

And a few seconds later, the door was opened by a man leaning heavily on a walker. I saw an oxygen container strapped to the walker, with a tube that divided into separate feeder lines going into his nostrils. This guy definitely was not in training for a marathon.

He was wearing a pair of shorts and a colored T shirt, along with sneakers with tabs, not laces. Eye glasses with thick lenses completed the picture of an old man.

"Mr. Binder?" I asked.

"Who wants to know?"

"My name is Will Jonas. And I want to talk to you about Abe Levy."

Binder started to shut the door, but I put my hand on it, and stopped its forward motion. Didn't take much pressure. The man was weak.

"I just want to ask you a few questions about the death of Abe Levy," I said, trying for a non-threatening tone of voice. "Please..."

Binder looked at me, then he sighed and shook his head.

"I don't want to think about this anymore. I just want to be left in peace. I'm a sick man. Can't you leave me alone?"

"Look," I said. "You knew Abe Levy, right? You visited him when he was in Vistas? No use denying it. I know you signed in as Smith or Jones or West."

"Irv's latest bright idea," Binder said sarcastically. "The older he gets, the crazier he gets."

He looked at me. The word, 'tired' was written all over his face.

"I told Irv. And I told Elliott – leave the damn thing alone. Nothing Abe says can mean anything to anyone. Nothing."

Binder shook his head.

"But no. Irv gets agitated easily these days. And he and Elliott

– they felt we had to keep checking."

Binder put one of his hands back on the door.

"Look, Mr. Jonas. I won't...I can't talk about any of this, anymore. I'm tired. I'm sick. The doctors tell me I'm on my way to congestive heart failure. So, just leave me alone, will you? Just leave me alone."

Binder tried again to close the door.

I didn't stop him.

Back in my car, I reviewed my brief talk with Binder.

What came across to me, was that this was a man who was tired of dealing with whatever Sherman, Freid and he were hiding. Whatever it was, that they were worried Abe Levy might have been saying -- might have been revealing in his dementia-related ramblings.

Obviously, at some point, I was going to have to pay a return visit to Binder. Push, to get more out of him.

In the meantime, I looked up Freid's address in my notes. It was 7134 Wish Avenue in a section of Encino known as Encino Village.

To get there, I went back to Winnetka, took it south to Victory, east on Victory to Topham, and then Topham for a few miles until I came to Aldea, where I turned right, then a quick left onto Bullock, which curved around to Wish Avenue. Number 7134 Wish was right there, at the curve.

There were fifty or so small homes in Encino Village, all built in the 1950's and early 1960's. They started at about 1,500 square feet, but a majority of them had been added to, by their owners.

Freid's house wasn't one of those. It was in its original form, but in nice shape. The exterior looked like it had been painted within the last few years, and the postage sized front yard and flower beds were well tended.

I parked, and started walking up toward the front door, wondering what I'd run into this time. Sherman-style belligerence? Or Binder's tired old man condition?

I didn't have to wait to find out. Before I reached the door, it was opened by a man whom I recognized as Freid. Unlike Binder, Freid looked like a vigorous guy, in good shape for someone in his 70's.

"You Jonas?" he shouted.

"Yes, and..."

I never got to finish my sentence.

"Then get the hell off my property!" he snarled, and he slammed the door shut.

Obviously, Sherman had called and alerted him.

I thought maybe I'd go the rest of the way up to the front door and ring the bell. Just to see what would happen. But I figured the end result would be zilch, so I gave it up. Two out of three is a pretty good batting average.

CHAPTER TWENTY

It was turning out to be a busy day.
When I got back to my office, Rose handed me her report on Edwin Nesbitt.

I'd asked her to find out two things. First, when did Nesbitt buy his new Mercedes? And second, what was he driving before that buy, and what happened to that car?
On the first point – when did Nesbitt buy his new Mercedes – it was in July of last year, just about six months after Abe Levy died.
And what about his old car?
According to what Rose had been able to find out, Nesbitt had filed a report with the police – a few days before he bought the Mercedes – that his car – a 1996 Honda Accord, had been stolen. It was never recovered.
Too many convenient coincidences here, I figured.

And one really big coincidence, which was – that Nesbitt reported his old car stolen – about the same time that Amos Clayton was killed in that hit and run.
So, let's think some more about this.

Suppose Nesbitt was the driver of that hit and run?

And he did it, *using his car!*

Now, what's he going to do about the damage to his car, when it slammed into Clayton's body?

Well, for starters, file a stolen vehicle report with the police.

Then -- and this was pure guessing on my part, but I felt pretty good about it – go down to one of the auto wrecking yards and bribe a crane operator to crush the Honda, along with all of the other cars he was crushing that day. Might take five hundred or so bucks, to convince the guy to do it, but totally doable, in my estimation.

Rose had been watching me as I read her report.

"What I found out – is it helpful?" she asked.

"Absolutely," I told her. "You're getting almost as good at this hacking stuff as Lu."

"What the women in your life do for you," Rose said with a smile.

"As it should be," I said.

"As it should be?" Rose repeated. "I need to tell Lu what you said."

"Our relationship – yours and mine – is on a confidential basis," I kidded. "So, you can't say anything to my wife."

"Okay," Rose laughed. And then she turned serious. "So, have you figured out yet, what happened to Abe Levy? Was he killed? Or did he die a natural death?"

"Not one hundred percent certain yet –but I am pretty sure he was killed."

Rose shook her head, and repeated something she had said to me, back when I first started on this case

"To kill a camp survivor. Someone who had already suffered so much. *That* is truly evil."

"Agreed," I told her.

I walked over to the closet in my office and took down a wooden box from the top shelf. I opened the box and took out the weapon stored there...a Ruger LCP along with its shoulder holster.

"You're going to see Nesbitt?" Rose asked.

"Uh huh." I said, putting on the holster, checking the Ruger to make sure the safety was on, and fitting the weapon into the holster. "Time for the man to answer some more questions."

I had Rose call over to Vistas, to see if Nesbitt was working today. He was, so I headed over there. When I arrived, I spoke to Ed Dworsky, and asked that he call Nesbitt to come to the conference room where I'd met the man before – without giving any advance notice that I'd be waiting for him.

Dworsky was reluctant to do so – understandably – but when I explained that what I was working on might end up being a police matter – then he went along with my request.

A couple of minutes later, Nesbitt came into the conference room.

When he saw me, he stopped. Then he turned and started to leave.

I said, "You better talk to me, Nesbitt, or you talk to the police next."

A bluff, but it worked.

Nesbitt stopped, then he came back into the room.

I was seated at the conference table and I motioned him to

take the seat across from me.

"What do you want?" Nesbitt asked, the defiance clear in his voice.

"Let's talk cars," I said. "Your old one. And your new one."

Nesbitt went rigid in his seat, but said nothing.

I continued.

"Kind of interesting to me, that one day, you report your seven-year-old Honda is stolen. And then a few days later, you buy that new, $40K+ Mercedes."

"So what?"

"So what happened to the Honda?"

"How should I know? It was stolen. I don't know what happened to it."

"You know what I think happened to it? I think it got banged up, when you ran over Amos Clayton."

That hit home. Nesbitt was shaken, but then, he managed to overcome his initial reaction. He said nothing.

I continued, "So then, I think you took it down to one of the car wrecking yards, and you bribed a crane operator to flatten it, along with all the other cars he was junking that day."

Nesbitt still said nothing, so I went on talking.

"Now, about that Mercedes — where'd you get the money to buy it? That's quite a stretch – from a seven-year-old, low-end Honda, to a top Mercedes model. Where'd the money come from?"

"That's none of your business," Nesbitt said.

He'd obviously come to a decision. He leaned across the table defiantly.

"Listen, Jonas –what you got is a bunch of nothing. Nada…What the lawyers call…circumstantial."

He stood up. "So I'm leaving. I don't have to talk to you. You're just a rent-a-cop."

CHAPTER TWENTY-ONE

Nesbitt was no dummy. He put his finger right on the two weaknesses in my investigation, thus far.

First, what I had *was* circumstantial. Good stuff. Logical stuff. But no hard evidence.

And second, I could paint myself any way I liked – private investigator...PI...ex-LAPD homicide detective – but I was what I was...and as Nesbitt put it... "Just a rent-a-cop."

Okay, time to bring Charlie up to date.

I needed some LAPD juice to get things into the next gear.

"Yeah, it sounds like it's about time to review all and let Klinger know what's happening," Charlie agreed.

And so, the next morning, the three of us – Captain Klinger, Charlie and I were seated in the Captain's office in the LAPD Devonshire station in Chatsworth.

Klinger was more than a little annoyed that the investigation had gone as far as it had, without him knowing about it. As I've pointed out before, the good Captain was a stickler for doing things by the book. And what I'd been doing, with Charlie's okay –sure wasn't in any book that he was used to reading.

But Klinger also had a long memory. And in that regard, I knew he was remembering how I'd saved his sister from being prosecuted several years earlier, in an insurance deal. She was an innocent, but stupid, player in that event. And if it wasn't for me, and how I got her out of it, she could have ended up in prison.

So, once he got over being pissed, Klinger listened to my summation of the case, thought some, and then asked me, "Will, what do really think? Do we have a case here?"

"Captain, do I think Levy was murdered? And do I think Amos Clayton was run over on purpose in that hit and run? And do I believe Nesbitt and Clayton were paid off? Yes, on all counts. I do think we have a case. But the hell of it is, I don't have any hard facts. And none of the suspects are in deep enough shit to bend over and admit to anything. Because, right now, we can't prove anything."

"The victim, Levy," Klinger mused, "The doctor signed off

okay on his death certificate. Easy enough to do, of course, if the doctor was crooked, and was paid off."

"Again," I said, "the facts are there. Clayton did get $10K in payments before he was run over in that hit and run. An unsolved hit and run."

"But no way to tie any of that together, right?" Klinger asked.

"Right," I admitted.

Klinger kept quiet for a moment, and then he asked his next question.

"That first victim...Levy, at the retirement home...do you think it would be worthwhile to get his body exhumed? To see if the coroner agrees with the natural causes via heart failure findings on the original death certificate? Or if he finds some hard evidence, that the death was not from natural causes?"

Charlie answered that one.

"Captain, Will and I wondered about that. Figured it would come up for discussion today, so I checked with the coroner's office. I asked them if they could determine if Levy died from natural causes, via heart failure. Or, if he was somehow killed? Most likely by being asphyxiated?"

"Here's what I was told."

"If, let's say, Nesbitt applied a pillow to Levy and asphyxiated him that way, it is possible there might not be any external signs of violence in someone as old as Levy and with his heart condition history. In other words, he wouldn't have put up much of a struggle, so no bruising. And, even if we did exhume the body now, a year plus after death, it would be unlikely that the signs of asphyxia would be present."

Klinger shook his head, and looking at his notes, he ticked off several points.

"We probably can't prove any homicide, even if we exhume the body."

"We've got nothing to nail anyone with, on the hit and run death."

"We can't prove that Nesbitt got rid of his car the way you've theorized."

"And Sherman gave you a reason – you might not like it, but it is a reason – why he and Freid and Binder signed in with those aliases."

Charlie answered, "All true, Captain. But we've won cases before, based on circumstantial evidence."

"Not ones as weak as this one," Klinger said.

I said, "Something is very clear to me, now, Captain. What we've got to do, is concentrate on finding the motive for all of this."

"What do you mean?" Klinger asked.

I continued.

"What I mean is, why have all of these things happened? What's been the cause? Up to now, I've been going on the theory, first given to me by Levy's granddaughter, that something happened in Auschwitz, involving the four of them – Sherman, Levy, Freid and Binder. And then, as he got deeper into his dementia, Levy kept talking about some killing. And I figured that's why Sherman, Freid and Binder kept checking on Levy. Because they were afraid he might reveal – I don't know – maybe some killing they'd done in the concentration camp?"

"But Rose keeps saying something that's beginning to make sense to me now. She keeps pointing out that you really can't blame people who came through those concentration camps, for whatever their behavior was. To a person, they were trying to survive. That's all they were doing. As Rose put it to me, 'If I'd been in Auschwitz, would I have acted differently? Trying every way I could to live? To survive?'"

"Okay, I can see that," Klinger agreed. "Not a nice thing, if it turns out those guys did some killing in the camp. But plenty of people would not blame them. And I'm not any expert on international law, but I kind of doubt if any government – today -- would try to extradite these guys and charge them with murder. It just wouldn't happen."

"So," I said, "we need to find the real motive here. The real reason why all of this stuff is happening."

Klinger didn't respond right away. Instead, he sat at his desk and tapped his pencil against the top of it, considering what I'd said. Then, he made his mind up.

"Okay, Will...you might have something there. To find the real motive."

He shook his head.

"But right now...I'm sorry, I don't see any reason for LAPD

to take over this investigation, and to go forward with it."

"You mean, we just stop?" Charlie asked.

Klinger smiled.

"I said, there is no investigation for LAPD to take forward."

He looked directly at me.

"But, Will, unless I've been asleep for the last…what is it, seven or eight years…you're not LAPD. So, if you want to keep going…"

I picked up on what Klinger was saying

"And if…once in a while…I wanted to discuss some things with my old partner…" I said.

"Well, who am I to do anything about that?" Klinger asked.

Our meeting with Klinger was over, and we left his office. Once out in the hall, Charlie asked, "You got any ideas on what to do next? Because I don't."

I nodded.

"A couple," I told him.

"What?"

"Well, for one thing, I want to go back and see Binder again. I'm guessing he's the weak one in that threesome of Sherman, Freid and himself. I want to try and work on him."

"You said, 'a couple,'" Charlie said.

"There's Nesbitt. I want to go at him again."

"He already told you where to get off, the last time you saw him."

"True. But that was when I was being a nice guy. And being concerned about how I acted, as almost some kind of an LAPD representative. This time around, no LAPD involvement. Just Nesbitt and me."

"Good luck on that one," Charlie said.

I never could fool Charlie, and I couldn't do so, now. What I said about Nesbitt? Words. Just words. Nesbitt had stonewalled me at our last meeting. And unless I had something new to hit him with, he'd do it again. Charlie knew it and I knew it.

"Okay," I admitted. "But there is one thing I do have to do."

"And that would be?"

"I need to bring Ally Morris up to date."

CHAPTER TWENTY-TWO

I called Ally Morris at her office, and she said she could come to my office late that same afternoon. So we set our meeting for 4:30 PM.

Ally arrived right on time. Obviously eager to hear what I had to say. I was sorry to disappoint her, but it couldn't be helped.

"What I have to tell you isn't very encouraging," I started out.

And then I gave her chapter and verse, right up to the LAPD decision about there being no actual case at the moment.

"You've found out so much," Ally protested. "How can the police not go after these people?"

"What we've got," I explained, "is what we call, 'circumstantial evidence.' In other words, it is logical evidence. Evidence that makes sense. But we don't have any hard facts to back things up."

"So what you're really saying is that you do think my grandfather was killed...but you have no way of proving it?"

"Unfortunately, that about describes it," I admitted.

"And I'm supposed to live with that?" she asked harshly. "Supposed to go along with the knowledge that my poor grandfather was murdered, and the people who did it, well...nothing happens to them?"

"Look, Ally, I'm going to keep working on this," I promised her.

"What's that supposed to mean?" she asked.

"It means I'm not giving up."

Ally looked at me. She shook her head. Was she angry? Frustrated? Discouraged? Just plain pissed off?

How about all of the above?

She said nothing. Then she stood and left my office.

Had I accomplished anything much for this granddaughter who thought her grandfather had been murdered?

What do you think?

CHAPTER TWENTY-THREE

The next morning, while I was in my office, plowing through files that Rose wanted me to review on some of our other cases, Louis called. You remember Louis the Fisherman...Snitch Extraordinaire?

"I got you all the goodies on Elite Trucking. Meet me in an hour, same place as last time." And he hung up.

That's all Louis said. He's not a believer in preliminaries, like 'hello' or end-of-call things like 'goodbye.'

So, here I was, an hour later, in my car, on the second floor of the parking garage at the Westfield Topanga mall, next to the elevator, and facing the Neiman Marcus sign. Hey, I can follow orders.

About thirty seconds later, the elevator doors opened, and there was Louis.

He swept the area with his eyes, then walked quickly over to my car and got in.

"Get on to Topanga and drive north," Louis said.

"And hello to you, too, Louis," I said, starting my car and heading for the ground floor and the Kittridge exit of the mall. At the exit, the traffic light was green, so I turned right, onto Topanga Canyon Boulevard.

"Okay, I'm on Topanga," I told Louis. "I'm heading north, and..." I looked in my rear view mirror..." There's your trail car. Everything's in order. So, what do you have?"

"I didn't turn up much," Louis said. "The background report you gave me, plus what you told me, gave me a pretty complete picture of Elite. But there was one thing I found – that wasn't in your report, and you didn't tell me about it, either. So maybe you don't know about it."

"What's that?"

"It's about the original owner – Richard Kohn."

"Yes," I said. "Sherman and Levy bought the company in 1961 from Kohn's wife. Kohn was dead."

"Yeah, but did you know what he died of?" Louis asked.

Obviously, Louis was having fun now, teasing me.

"No, but you're going to tell me, aren't you?"

"Kohn was shot to death, also in 1961, about eight months before Sherman and Levy bought the company."

I damn near drove through the red light at Saticoy!

"What? How'd it happen? Who was responsible?"

"The details I know are these," Louis ticked them off. "The case was never solved. No one was ever caught. From what I was able to find out – it looked like a robbery gone wrong."

Louis paused for a moment, checked a piece of paper he was holding, and then he continued.

"This might also be interesting to you. Kohn, Sherman and Levy all were in that German concentration camp you mentioned to me. Auschwitz."

Up ahead, on the right, there was a RightAid drug store.

Louis said, "End of report, Will."

He pointed at the drug store.

"Nice doing business with you, again. Pull into the Right Aid parking lot. I'll get out, then you continue, around and out the back of the lot."

CHAPTER TWENTY-FOUR

I hurried back to my office and called Charlie Black.

When he answered, I said, "Motive, Charlie. I got a real motive."

Right away, Charlie caught on. Just like when we were partners working homicides. A word or two from either of us, and the other knew what it meant.

"Details!" he demanded.

"Okay. Like I said when we met with Klinger, I was starting to feel that silencing Abe Levy because of something that happened in Auschwitz...that was not enough of a motive to kill him."

"But how about this? How about the original owner of Elite Trucking – Richard Kohn —being murdered? And then eight months later, Sherman and Levy buy the company? And how about this fact? Like Sherman and Levy — along with Freid and Binder — Kohn was in Auschwitz."

"Big, big coincidences," Charlie said, the excitement building in his voice. "And we don't believe in coincidences."

"Therefore," I continued, "when Levy, in his dementia, started talking about — 'the killing...the killing' – this definitely could be something for Sherman and Freid and Binder to worry about. Because this 'killing' may not have been about something that happened in Auschwitz."

"But it could be about the killing of Kohn," Charlie picked up the thought, "which took place right here. In the U.S. Where homicide cases are never closed."

"So," I said, "if Levy's rantings were to draw some police attention, then the three of them would be right to worry about an investigation... coming...right...at...them!"

"Charlie," I said, "we need to review the original file. See if these guys were questioned – in 1961 – when Kohn was murdered. Obviously, none of them were charged at that time."

"Doesn't necessarily mean they're innocent," Charlie said. "Just means they weren't caught – that time around."

"When can you get the file?" I asked.

"Not sure. I'll get on it right away. And I need to bring

Klinger up to date on this."

"Of course," I agreed.

"Will, I hope we still have that file. We're talking about a cold case that goes back...42 years."

CHAPTER TWENTY-FIVE

As soon as I finished talking to Charlie, Rose came into my office. She looked grim.

"What's up?" I asked.

"Sherman is up," she said. "He's way up there, in anger and shouting and threatening."

"What do you mean?"

Rose pointed at my phone.

"Find out for yourself. He's on the phone. Waiting to talk to you. And he is very aggravated. Because Ally Morris went to see him at Elite."

"Uh, oh."

"Yes, uh, oh."

Rose pointed at my phone again.

"Go," she directed. "Pick up the phone and listen to the meshuganah."

This was another Yiddish word Rose had taught me over our years together, so I knew that a meshuganah was someone who was very angry...mad about something that's happened. Get the picture?

I picked up the phone.

"Mr. Sherman...this is Will Jonas. What can I do for you?"

"You can keep that bitch from coming to my office and accusing me of killing her grandfather," he shouted into my ear.

"She shows up here. She barges in. She makes that accusation. And she tells me that you told her it was so. What the hell kind of crap are you shoveling out, Jonas! You better get her to stop saying things like that. And you better stop feeding her this kind of information."

Although I didn't like being on the receiving end of Sherman's anger – actually – I was kind of pleased. Because it was confirming to me that he was beginning to come apart at the seams. If Ally could shake him up so much – well – how about his being told that the LAPD was re-opening the Kohn case? That really should give a dose of heavy-duty internal upset to Sherman, and to Freid and Binder, as well.

Of course, I wasn't sure about this last point yet. Charlie still had to get the file, we needed to review it, and then we needed to plead the case with Klinger, as to whether Charlie could activate the case, and start questioning Sherman and the others.

But, I decided I'd ignore that point for now, and apply some more heat to Sherman's feet.

"I'll talk to Ms. Morris," I said.

I paused, and then I added, "Oh. You might like to know that, because of some new developments I've found, the police are reviewing the Richard Kohn case. You know, when Kohn was shot to death, during that supposed robbery? Back in 1961?"

Sherman took a few seconds to respond. And when he did, his voice was soft, but what he said was aimed at me like a laser.

"You are heading for trouble, Jonas. Guaranteed."

CHAPTER TWENTY-SIX

"So how could you possibly take it on yourself to go and see Irving Sherman?" I asked Ally Morris the next morning, when I reached her at her office.

"How did you know about that?" she asked.

"Because Sherman called me and raised holy hell about what you said to him…about killing your grandfather! And he blames me for, as he put it…'feeding her that information.'"

"Well," Ally said defensively, "I was frustrated. Nothing is happening. Nothing at all!"

"Ally," I said, trying to sound as calm as possible, "you are not helping things with a stunt like that. You are alerting Sherman, and the others, that we are actively investigating them. And when they know this, it becomes even harder to deal with them."

I heard a sigh at the other end of the phone.

"I guess I sort of…went off…the deep end," she admitted.

"The deep end is right," I told her.

"Will," Ally asked, "how is this going to turn out? Is anything going to come of it?"

I didn't want to tell Ally about the Kohn killing that Charlie and I had just discussed. Hopefully, she'd learned her lesson. But still, I decided that the less she knew at the moment, the better.

However, I did want to give her something to hope for, so I said, "Listen. We're working on some more developments. It's progress. Believe me. This investigation is not over yet."

"Do you really have some new developments?" Rose asked, after I ended my call with Ally Morris.

Rose had been in my office, sorting some files, while I was on the phone with Ally.

I told Rose about my meeting with Louis and about my phone discussion with Charlie.

"So," she said, "it could be that this Sherman and the other two, killed Kohn, another Auschwitz survivor?"

"Not sure, but it could be," I confirmed.

"So bad. So bad," Rose said.

CHAPTER TWENTY-SEVEN

Charlie called me late in the afternoon, to let me know the Kohn murder case file had been located, and he'd have it, tomorrow afternoon.

I decided I'd use the time between now and then, to try for additional sessions with two people I considered to be, to use the police term, "Persons of interest."

First on my list was the retirement home attendant, Edwin Nesbitt.

I wanted to talk to Nesbitt in his home, rather than at Vistas, in case the meeting got ugly.

I didn't have Nesbitt's home address, so I called Ed Dworsky at Vistas, to get it.

After we exchanged hellos, Dworsky said, "Evidently, Nesbitt has quit on me. He didn't report in for his shift two days ago. We've called him at home, but no response. Haven't heard a word from him.

"And now, here you are again. Tell me, does Nesbitt's disappearance have anything to do with those pictures you said Abe Levy wanted to give to his friends from Auschwitz?"

"In a way...yes."

"In a way, yes," Dworsky repeated. "Now, what does that mean?"

It was time to be honest with Dworsky. I was convinced that whatever had happened to Levy, Dworsky had nothing to do with it.

I said to him, "When I came to Vistas, I was just starting to investigate the possibility that Abe Levy did not die...a natural death."

There was a pause, while Dworsky absorbed this information.

"You mean...you mean that he was...killed?"

"I'm leaning toward that."

"But Dr. Clayton signed the death certificate. Natural causes and heart failure."

"Clayton and Nesbitt may have been in this, together. Possible homicide. Then falsifying the death certificate."

"But why?"

MANIFESTO/YOU REMEMBER…YOU DIE

"That's something I'm not sure of, yet. That's still something I'm trying to figure out."

There was another pause before Dworsky spoke again.

"Will, am I in trouble here? Is Vistas in trouble?" he asked, the worry evident in his voice. "Shit! What a mess. I try like hell to run a good place here. To make Vistas a fine retirement home!"

"Ed," I assured Dworsky, "Nesbitt and Clayton were a couple of bad eggs in your otherwise fine place. I see it that way. And if this becomes an official police matter, then I will do all I can to make sure the LAPD sees it that way. And I'm pretty sure I can do that."

"God, I hope so! I love this place. And aside from the business implications, I'd personally be devastated if this affected us badly."

"Not going to happen, if I can help it, Ed," I assured him.

Then I asked him, "I assume you have Nesbitt's home address. Can you please give it to me?"

Dworsky sighed. "Well, I wonder if I should? I mean, what about Nesbitt coming after me, for disclosing that information?" He laughed, only there was no humor in it. "But hey, if he's in the kind of trouble you're saying, I don't think I have to worry, about giving you his address. Hold on, and I'll get it for you."

CHAPTER TWENTY-EIGHT

The address Dworsky gave me for Nesbitt was 8031 Owensmouth, Unit 6, Chatsworth, a multi-unit, rental complex, a few blocks north of Parthenia. Took me about twenty minutes to get there.

I parked and walked to the front of the building. The entry was open, so I went in and walked down the hall to Unit 6, which was toward the rear on the first of the two floors.

The door was open and I walked in.

A man was mopping the kitchen floor.

"You here to look at the unit?" he asked. "It'll be cleaned up and ready, in about an hour."

"I'm looking for Edwin Nesbitt," I told him.

"Me, too," the man said. "He's skipped...and he owes me a month's rent."

"You the manager?"

"Yes. And you are...?"

"Will Jonas," I said.

"He owe you money, too?" the manager asked, sourly.

"No. I just want to talk to him. Any idea where he went?"

"If I knew, I'd go after him," the manager said.

He shook his head.

"Nah. I don't know. He just took off, in that jazzy new Mercedes he had. Hey, I wonder if he skipped out on some payments there, too?"

CHAPTER TWENTY-NINE

As I exited Nesbitt's building, I called Charlie on my cell phone.

"I've got two new developments in our investigation," I said.

"And they are...?" he prompted.

"First, Edwin Nesbitt, the Vistas attendant who took care of Abe Levy, stopped showing up for work a couple of days ago."

"And second, he's vacated his apartment, skipping out, without paying his rent."

"Thus, meaning," Charlie picked up, "that he's running."

"That's the way I see it."

"Okay, that gives me enough to put out an all points on him. I'll have to clear it with Klinger, since we haven't officially opened up the case, but he'll go along on this."

"Remember, Nesbitt bought that new Mercedes recently, so DMV will have his license plate number on hand."

"Yeah, we'll be getting that. What are you up to, next?"

"I'm going to see Ben Binder again. Try and break him down. He was kind of weak, the last time I saw him. Pretty sick, physically. And seemed very tired of the whole thing, mentally. I'm hoping I can squeeze something out of him."

About a half hour later, when I rang Ben Binder's doorbell, I got a "twofer."

Elliott Freid opened it.

"You again," he said. He shook his head. "You just won't go away, will you?"

Unlike the last time I'd seen him, when Freid invited me to get the hell off my property," this time, he was less combative.

Freid turned and walked down the hall.

"You might as well come in," he said over his shoulder.

I followed him into the living room.

Ben Binder was seated there, half reclining in a lounger chair. Dressed the same as last time. Shorts and a T shirt, sneakers with tabs, glasses with thick lenses. He was connected to the oxygen tank, with the tubes running into his nostrils.

If anything, Binder looked more worn out than he had, just a few days ago. I remembered him telling me about his congestive heart failure condition. It looked to me like the situation was worsening.

"How are you feeling?" I asked, trying to start things off in a friendly way.

"Cut the crap," Freid said. "What do you want?"

Binder raised his hand toward Freid.

"Elliott, enough," he said. "I'm tired. Tired of the whole thing. And even though you don't want to admit it, so are you. So are you."

"Tired of covering for Irving Sherman?" I asked, hoping to get a wedge in there, trying to separate them from Sherman.

"We owe everything to Irv!" Freid said strongly. "He was the one who held us together. Who gave us the will to keep going, when we were in the camp. Without him, we wouldn't have made it." He looked at Binder. "We need to remember that, Ben. We need to remember that."

Binder sighed.

"Elliott, I do remember. And I am grateful. But that was a different Irv, then. Today, though? He's more with the emotions. With the agitation. He's a different person today. He's gotten old, Elliott. He's gotten old."

"What you need to consider," I cut in, "is that there are three killings here. And they are going to be investigated by the police. And when that happens, you both better be on the right side."

"What three killings?" Binder asked, the concern evident in his voice.

"For one, I'm talking about the death of Abe Levy."

"There was no killing there," Freid said. "Irv told us the death certificate said it was natural causes. That's what the doctor wrote."

"That's in doubt now," I said. "Even to the point where Levy's body may be exhumed and a new autopsy done."

Yeah, so I was stretching the truth. But all in a good cause, right?

This news clearly shook up both Binder and Freid.

Then I followed up with... "And about the doctor who signed the death certificate? Well, he was killed in a hit and run about six months ago. And the police are investigating that, to see if it ties back in to Levy's death.

"What are you talking about?" Binder asked. "I don't know anything about that."

"Nor do I," Freid said.

So then I gave them the real zinger.

"And, it looks like the LAPD is going to re-open that killing of Richard Kohn, back in 1961. You both remember that one, don't you?"

Binder slumped down in his lounger, looking like he wanted to find some way to hide in the chair's cushions.

Freid was also hit hard by this news. But he recovered, and looked across at Binder. Freid shook his head at Binder-- seemed to me in a cautionary way — then he turned to me.

"You have to leave now. We don't have anything more to say to you."

I stared at him for a moment, then spoke to Binder.

"Nothing more to say?" I asked. "You feel the same way?"

Freid stepped between Binder and me.

"Time to leave," he said again. "Now. Out."

I did an exaggerated shrug.

"Well, if that's the way you guys want to play it. Okay...But once LAPD gets into it, and they will, you're going to be on the losing side. Think about that."

I looked at Binder. If being worried was measured on a scale of 1 to10, with 10 being the most worried...well...Binder looked to be about a 12.

As for Freid? More like an 8.

CHAPTER THIRTY

All this running around makes for a tired and hungry guy. So, the smell of some good cooking, when I got home that evening, was great.

"Marinated Butterflied Lamb. That's what you're smelling," Lu announced, as she greeted me with a kiss and the usual glass of chilled club soda, poured over ice.

"Now that's something I've never had before," I said, as we walked into the living room and sat on the couch. "You are really getting into this cooking shtick."

"It's not a 'shtick,'" Lu said, poking me in the ribs. "I told you I was going to become an accomplished chef, and tonight is just another example of how I'm progressing."

About an hour later, I assured Lu that, "You've reached your 'accomplished chef' goal. This was some great dish! Thank you. Thank you. Thank you."

"You're welcome," Lu said. "Now, tell me about your day. Any progress on the 'who killed grandpa'" mystery?"

"Getting close," I said. "Meeting tomorrow with Charlie and Klinger. The end result may well be that LAPD takes over the investigation and starts looking into not only Abe Levy's death a year ago, but also the death in 1961 of a Richard Kohn, the owner of Elite Trucking. That's the company owned by my chief suspect in all of this...Irving Sherman."

"Wow," Lu said. "That's a spread of...42 years."

"That it is. And the problem in all of this remains...no hard facts. Lots of circumstantial and logical information. But like they say, 'no smoking gun.'"

"Speaking of smoking guns..." Lou said.

She looked at me and grinned. Then, she fluttered her eyelids in an exaggerated way.

She got my complete attention.

I stood up, walked over to her side of the table, and kissed her.

Lu doubled my kiss in return.

Now, I ask you...who needs Viagra? When there's Marinated Butterflied Lamb?

CHAPTER THIRTY-ONE

The next afternoon, Charlie and I met with Captain Klinger in Klinger's office, at the LAPD Devonshire Station, to review the file on the 1961 killing of Richard Kohn at his office in Elite Trucking.

Klinger told me, "Will, there's a copy here for you, of the 1961 file."

He turned to Charlie.

"But Charlie, since you've already reviewed the file, for the purpose of this meeting, let's have you give us the key facts."

Charlie looked at his notes.

"Okay, first the crime scene. Kohn was shot in his office at Elite. Between 8 and 9PM, the coroner figured. Same office, same building as where the company still is located, in Canoga Park on Canoga Avenue."

"Shot twice with a Smith & Wesson. The weapon was never recovered."

"Lots of fingerprints of many, many people – as might be expected – but no suspicious prints turned up."

"Evidence of a struggle between Kohn and his assailant. Papers knocked off of Kohn's desk and onto the floor. A small coffee table in front of the couch upended. Some bruising on Kohn's face and body, which the coroner said could be consistent with someone hitting the victim."

"Kohn's wallet was missing. No idea how much was in it, but his wife said he usually had several hundred dollars with him."

"Also missing was a Rolex wristwatch. The man had expensive tastes. His wife said she thought it had cost about six or seven thousand dollars – although she wasn't sure."

"All Elite employees were interviewed. All alibis checked out. I looked especially for the alibis of Sherman, Levy, Freid and Binder. Their wives all said their husbands were at home, at the time the killing took place. And just to anticipate one of your questions, all four of the wives are now dead. No chance there, to re-question."

"The detective in charge of the investigation was a Phil McManus. And in my opinion, he did a good and thorough job.

95

But nothing turned up."

"McManus ended his investigation by describing the case as a homicide occurring during a robbery. He classified it as unsolved. And that's been its status ever since."

After Charlie finished, no one spoke, as we all sorted through what Charlie had told us. Finally, I started the discussion.

"I hate to say it…but we still don't have enough concrete evidence. Damn it! I am sure, as I sit here, that both Levy and Kohn were murdered! And for that matter, Dr. Clayton, too."

Charlie picked up on what I'd said.

"Will, you said, 'we don't have *enough* concrete evidence.' "What concrete evidence do you think we *do* have?"

I answered him.

"The fact that the home attendant –Nesbitt – has skipped town. Why would he do that, unless he was afraid we'd find out that Levy didn't die of natural causes? If that proved out, then he'd be the prime suspect for Levy's murder, right?"

"And then there's Doctor Clayton. His wife told me about the $10K he received. Why else would he have gotten that money, if not to falsify Levy's death certificate?"

"And to me, the biggest clue of all, is the Kohn killing. A killing that… eight months later…made it possible for Sherman and Levy to take over a successful business that made them plenty solvent for many years."

"And finally, here's something that isn't concrete evidence, but it's something I really believe. Ben Binder is close to cracking. I've been to see him twice. He's weak. He's sick. Hell…he's dying. A little more pressure, and I think he *will* crack."

I stopped talking for a few seconds, as I lined up my final thoughts.

"Okay, here's what I think we do next."

"Captain, I think you should open up this case, and as step one, invite Sherman in for a discussion. He'll probably come lawyered up—but I don't care."

"Because what I'd like to do, is call Luis Rivera at the Times, and let him know about Sherman being brought in for questioning about a 41-year-old cold case, and the potential connection to two other murders within the last year."

"And I'd give Luis enough background, so he'd have a good

story to write, the day after Sherman is brought in. You know…'Prominent Local Businessman Being Questioned About 41-year-old Unsolved Murder. Associates Also May Be Questioned."

"And at the same time, I'd alert Jennifer Dawn at Channel Five, and suggest she be outside the building, so she can try and question Sherman when he comes out, after his session with Charlie. It would be great if she can get some 'camera in your face' coverage for the six and eleven o'clock newscasts."

"Because what you're hoping." Charlie said, "Is that the pressure of the publicity in the Times and on Channel Five might make one of them crack…or more specifically…make Ben Binder crack."

"Exactly!" I agreed. "Binder's the weak link. If Freid hadn't been with Binder yesterday, then I think Binder might have cracked, then."

Charlie and I looked at Klinger. After a pause, he nodded.

"Okay, Charlie, do bring Sherman in for questioning. Activate the Richard Kohn homicide case. And broaden your inquiry to include your questioning Sherman about the Levy and Clayton deaths, too."

Klinger paused again.

"Will…as for the Times and Channel Five…that's not something we'd do."

He shook his head.

"But as I told you before, you're not LAPD. So, I certainly can't control you…"

Klinger left the rest of his sentence unsaid.

I nodded my understanding.

CHAPTER THIRTY-TWO

When I was still on the Job, Luis Rivera, the crime reporter for the Los Angeles Times and I, became...if not friends...at least, good acquaintances... who recognized the value of helping each other, for the benefit of both of us.

To explain, Luis might ask me for "unidentified source" information that he needed, in order to add some necessary "meat" to a story he was writing.

And there were times, when I'd give Luis an advance tip about an investigation that was going to be newsworthy.

We both recognized the value of our relationship.

My information and tips helped Luis build and keep his reputation as the best crime reporter in Southern California – and for that matter, one of the best in the country.

And if I could provide enough reliable information, then Luis was willing to write a story that would help me in one way or another.

Like now – when my objective was to put the heat on Sherman and the others.

Luis and I met shortly after my meeting with Klinger and Charlie ended. I gave him a full rundown on what I'd learned about the Levy and Clayton killings, and our growing suspicions about the Richard Kohn murder in 1961.

Luis said he'd need some time to do his own checking, but he figured he'd be ready to file his story, right after Sherman was brought in for questioning. In other words, it would be ideal for Sherman to be brought in, during the morning, then Luis could do his story for the edition that came out the following morning.

As for Jennifer Dawn at Channel Five, we'd built up the same sort of relationship, over the years. And here, too, the results had been mutually beneficial.

So after I gave Jennifer chapter and verse on the situation, she had to fight hard not to salivate, as she pictured herself – on live tv – shoving a mike in Sherman's face and asking him what he knew about the deaths of Kohn, Levy and Clayton?

I promised both Luis and Jennifer, that I'd alert them, just as soon as I learned, when Charlie was able to schedule having

Sherman to come in to the Station.

CHAPTER THIRTY-THREE

Charlie managed to set up the session with Irving Sherman for 10AM, two mornings after he, Klinger and I had our meeting. I alerted Luis and Jennifer, and that morning, I joined Klinger in the observation room, that gave us a view into the interrogation room where Charlie would be interviewing Sherman.

Promptly at 10 AM, Sherman and his attorney arrived at the Station. Charlie met them at the front desk and escorted them into the interrogation room.

"Let it be noted, Detective Black," Sherman's lawyer, Kenneth McGuire said, once they were seated, "that Mr. Sherman does not intend to say anything, until you explain to us, why he has been directed to appear here."

"So noted, Counselor," Charlie said. "Let it also be noted that we are filming and recording this interview." He then went on to do the introductory ID formalities. After completing them, Charlie began his interrogation.

"Mr. Sherman, we have asked you to come in today, so that we could discuss several matters. First, let's talk about your friend and former partner, Abraham Levy, and his death a year ago. We have reason to believe that the death certificate, claiming that death was via natural causes, and from a failed heart —well, the death certificate was falsified, and Mr. Levy was killed."

"My client will not have any comment on that," McGuire interrupted. "Next, please."

Charlie of course wasn't surprised. It was what we had expected would happen. So, he went on to the next topic.

"We also would like to talk to you, Mr. Sherman, about the hit and run death of Dr. Amos Clayton, the physician who completed the Levy death certificate."

"Detective Black, my client will not have any comment," McGuire said again. "Next, please."

Again, Charlie wasn't surprised. He continued.

"And we would like to talk to you about the death of Richard Kohn in 1961."

As expected, McGuire jumped in again.

"Detective Black, my client will not have any comment,"

McGuire repeated.

Charlie said nothing further, and after a few seconds, McGuire spoke again.

"Detective, if you have no further questions, then Mr. Sherman and I will now leave. And may I point out to you that we do not appreciate the kind of baseless harassment Mr. Sherman has been subjected to, here today."

"For the future, any inquiries you have of Mr. Sherman -- you direct them to me, rather than to him. Do I make myself clear?"

"Perfectly."

McGuire stood up and nodded to Sherman to also stand.

"Well, then, Detective Black," McGuire said, "Mr. Sherman and I will now be leaving."

As McGuire and Sherman were getting ready to leave, I quickly exited the observation room and hurried just outside the Stationhouse, to where Jennifer Dawn was standing, with her cameraman.

"He's coming," I told her, and I went to stand beside her.

McGuire and Sherman came out the door, and as I hoped, Sherman saw me.

Before Jennifer could ask her opening question, Sherman, his face contorted in anger, bulled his way to standing right in front of me, almost nose to nose.

"You!" he shouted. "You're behind this! And I'm going to make you pay, you son of a bitch! You're going to be very, very sorry!"

"Irv, stop!" McGuire said loudly, grabbing Sherman by the arm and trying to pull him away from me and from the tv camera.

At which point, Jennifer shoved her way to directly in front of Sherman.

"Mr. Sherman," she shouted, "what can you tell us about the death of Richard Kohn in 1961? And the death last year of Abraham Levy?"

"No comment!" McGuire shouted. "No comment!" he repeated, as he grabbed Sherman by his arm and rushed him down the steps to their waiting car.

Jennifer, bless her "breaking news" heart, followed them down, repeating Sherman's name and asking her question –to which, of course, she got no answers. All on camera!

When the car took off, Jennifer turned to me. But I didn't want to go on camera. Anything I'd say would be anti-climactic. I was happy, because Sherman had acted exactly how Charlie and I had hoped he would.

The critical time in all of this would be tomorrow morning. When the Times came out with Rivera's story, and Channel Five was still running the tape of the encounter between Sherman and me. And I was betting, too, that the other local tv news shows would have cobbled together their own stories by then.

But my big bet was this: that Ben Binder would see the Times and the tv coverage – and it would be enough to get him to turn. That's what I was hoping. And that's why I was planning to be at Binder's apartment, knocking on his front door, early tomorrow morning.

CHAPTER THIRTY-FOUR

The next morning, here was the headline in Luis Rivera's Los Angeles Times story:

Police Question Prominent Business Executive About 41-Year-Old Unsolved Homicide

The story then went on to identify Irving Sherman as the business executive, and it reported that he was being questioned about the unsolved homicide of Richard Kohn, in 1961, as well as the recent deaths of Abraham Levy and Doctor Amos Clayton.

As for Chanel Five, it kept showing that encounter between Sherman and me, and his threatening me. And then it showed Jennifer Dawn, running after Sherman, with her repeated question… "What can you tell us about the death of Richard Kohn in 1961? And the death last year of Abraham Levy?"

All in all, the Times and Channel Five came out pretty much the way I was hoping. And that was good.

But what I was *really* hoping, was that the publicity would have an impact on Ben Binder. Make him see the need to cooperate.

And it was with that hope, that I once again rang the doorbell to unit #21 in the Georgian Arms.

It took some time, but then the door was opened, and Binder looked out at me.

"You," he said, the strain of events obvious in how he looked and the softness of his voice. "I figured you'd show up. Are you proud of what you did to Irv yesterday? I spoke to him early this morning. He's very agitated. Very upset."

"Just trying to get to the truth," I answered. "Can I come in?"

Binder moved his walker back from the door.

"Can I stop you?" he asked wearily.

He turned his walker and shuffled back toward the living room.

I came in, closed the door, and followed him.

Binder lowered himself into his lounger. Then he looked at me and shook his head.

"We owe so much to Irv. I mean me. And Elliott. And yes,

Abe Levy. None of us would have made it through the camps without Irv pushing us, helping us, making us want to survive."

He paused and then leaned forward for emphasis.

"And now you're doing this to the man? He's a wreck. From that story. That television news. I never heard him so angry, as he was this morning, on the telephone!"

"Look," I said, "Sherman obviously was wonderful for all of you. But...I don't know what's happened. And I don't guess you do, either. But the way he's acting now? Well...you have to think about what it's best for you to do."

Binder looked defiantly at me.

"Elliott and I do not know anything about Abe Levy supposedly being killed. All we know... is that Irv told us... Abe died a natural death."

"And as far as this...Dr. Clayton...we don't know anything about what happened to him. We only know his name, because Irv told us he was the doctor who signed Abe's death certificate."

"What about Richard Kohn?" I asked. "Do you know anything about his death? Did Sherman ever talk to you about that one?"

"I know a little bit about it," Binder admitted.

"And what would that be?" I prodded.

"Irv never said anything to Elliott or me, about him shooting Richard Kohn. But he was worried that he might come under suspicion. Because he and Kohn had a big argument the day before Kohn was killed. Kohn had promised Irv a share of the company. Making him an owner. Something Irv wanted very badly. But it didn't happen, and Richard and Irv had that big argument."

"So, Sherman asked us – Abe, Freid and me – not to tell the police that he and Richard had their big argument. Irv was worried that would lead the police to think he'd killed Kohn."

I pressed.

"So, neither Freid nor you, ever heard Sherman admit to shooting Kohn?"

"No we didn't."

I sat back and did some thinking.

What Binder had given me up to now, wasn't that good. Supposedly, he and Freid knew nothing about the killing of

Richard Kohn – other than the fact that Sherman had asked them not to tell the police about the argument he and Kohn had.

And on Levy's death? If I'm to believe Binder, then he and Freid thought Levy died of natural causes – because – that's what Sherman told them.

I'd have to check all this against what Freid would tell me – he needed to be next on my list to see today – but I had a suspicion the information would be about the same.

In other words, I had to admit to myself – I really didn't have much more than I had before yesterday –even with all of the press coverage this morning.

Of course, I reminded myself, there was still more questioning that should be done of Sherman – but based on how his lawyer was stonewalling yesterday, I didn't see anything good coming up there.

I was about to ask Binder some more questions, when my cell phone rang.

It was Charlie.

"Will..." he began.

"Charlie," I interrupted, "I'm with Ben Binder. I'll call you back shortly."

"No!" Charlie shouted. "Listen. Sherman's in your office. He's got Rose. He's armed. And he says he'll shoot her, unless you come back to your office! Now!"

CHAPTER THIRTY-FIVE

I didn't know it, but Charlie, after he called me, went to his desk sergeant and they located a black and white that was cruising on Winnetka, right near Binder's apartment. The car was given orders to clear the way and escort me back to my office.

I found this out when, shortly after leaving Binder's apartment, as I was barreling south on Winnetka, a black and white came up behind me, lights flashing.

I started to curse, and began slowing down. But the car pulled up next to me, and the officer in the passenger seat signaled for me to follow. I got the idea, and fell into line.

A short ride later, we reached the two story building in Warner Center in Woodland Hills, where my office was located, on the first floor.

Several black and whites, lights flashing, surrounded the main entry to the building, and I also saw a SWAT truck.

I nosed my car in toward the building entrance. Charlie came running toward me. I stopped, got out, and ran to meet him.

"What's going on?" I shouted.

"Here's what we know," Charlie answered.

"About a half hour ago, we got a 911 call from a lady who also has an office in your building. It's on the first floor, down at the other end of the building. But the ladies rest room is about at the mid-point of the building. And this lady was coming out of that room, when she saw a man, walking very quickly toward your office. His back was to her. But when he turned and reached out with one hand, to open your door, she saw him hold up his other hand and aim a gun at the door. She was sure that's what she saw. So she ran into her office and called 911."

"How do you know it's Sherman?"

"Because just a couple of minutes after the 911 call, I got a call from Rose, with Sherman on the line, too. She told me Sherman was there, and that he wanted you to come into the office. At which point, Sherman grabbed the phone and said that if you didn't show up, he'd kill Rose."

I nodded toward the SWAT truck.

"What are they figuring?"

"Nothing definite yet. They have someone trying to see if they have a shot through one of the windows into your office. That's where they're at right now."

"How do you know that Rose and Sherman are in *my* office, and not in the outer office, where Rose sits?"

"Because your Rose is one smart and cool lady. When she called, she said – 'we are in Will's own office'... In other words, she made sure we'd know exactly where they were."

Way to go, Rose!

"Okay," I asked Charlie, "have you had any more communication with Sherman or Rose?"

"I spoke to Sherman a couple of minutes ago. To let him know you were on your way here."

"What'd he say?"

"He said you better get here fast...or else..."

"What kind of communication setup do you have into my office?"

"Come on. I'll show you."

Charlie ran toward the building entrance and I followed.

Just inside the entrance, a small table had been set up with a phone line, both outgoing and receiving, plus a loudspeaker.

Jim Raditch, one of the LAPD negotiator specialists was seated at the table. When he saw me, he stood up and indicated I should sit down. Covering the phone, Radich told me, "I just talked to Sherman. He's threatening to kill Rose, if you don't come into the office in the next five minutes."

"Let me talk to him," I said.

Raditch flipped a switch and nodded for me to go ahead.

"Mr. Sherman," I said, "This is Will Jonas."

"You sonofabitch!" Sherman shouted. "You better come in! Now! Alone! And you better not be carrying a gun!"

"Hey," I said softly, trying to calm things down, "Rose has nothing to do with this. It's between you and me. Why don't you let her go? And then I'll come in."

"Nothing doing! You better come in! Now!"

Rose shouted, "Will, he has a gun. He'll shoot you!"

"You shut up!" Sherman roared. "You shut the hell up!"

I covered the phone line and turned to Charlie. "I have to go in."

"He'll kill you. You'll be like a duck in a pond."

"Yeah, but I can't let him hurt Rose."

I went back to the phone line.

"Sherman, I want to come in. But since you won't let Rose go, at least let her sit behind my desk. I want her out of the way of any trouble. What about that? Okay for her to go and sit behind my desk?"

There were several seconds of silence.

Then Sherman spoke.

"Okay, Lady, go and sit down behind his desk. And make it fast."

After a few seconds, I asked, "Rose, are you behind the desk?"

"Yes, Will," she answered.

I stood up and took off my shoulder holster, which held my Ruger LCP. No way could I wear the holster, going in there. I wanted to carry the Ruger in my hand, hidden behind my back as long as possible.

Charlie put a bullet proof vest on me. I wasn't confident about how much good the vest would do, especially from a close-up shot. And especially if the shot was to my head, or arms or legs. But it would be better than nothing.

I spoke to Sherman again.

"Okay," I told him, "I'm going to come in, now."

"Unarmed, Jonas!" Sherman shouted. "No gun!"

"No gun!" I shouted back.

I started walking down the hall toward my office.

Did I have a plan in mind, for what to do, once I reached there?

The best I could come up with, was this.

I'd step into Rose's outer office. I'd go down low and get to the wall next to the door to my office. Then, I'd reach over and turn the knob so the door wasn't engaged. Then I'd shove the door open as hard as I could, so that it would swing back and bang against the wall.

Hopefully, that action might startle Sherman and he'd take a shot at the entryway. What I'd do then, was stay low, slide into the room, and fire at Sherman. I figured he'd be standing to the right of my desk, as I faced into the office. This would be away from Rose, who, hopefully, was behind my desk, out of the line of fire.

Much of a plan? No.

The best I could come up with? Yes.

I got ready.

I started to go into Rose's office.

Then I heard Sherman cry out... "What the...!"

Two shots were fired!

To hell with my plan!

I ran through Rose's office, slammed open the door to my office, and went in, my weapon held in front, ready to fire.

But there was no need for any further action.

I saw Sherman on the floor, blood flowing out of his right shoulder, his weapon also on the floor, a few feet away. The wound looked serious, but not critical.

And I saw Rose.

Standing behind my desk.

Pointing my Glock 19 at Sherman.

Bless that little old lady!

She'd remembered what I had *not* remembered – that when I wasn't using it, I kept the Glock in the top right drawer of my desk.

I'd forgotten.

But Rose, as soon as she sat down at my desk – she remembered.

And somehow, when Sherman was watching the door into my office, waiting for me to come in, Rose had managed to get the Glock out of the drawer, and to disengage the safety.

"Sherman must have heard me fumbling with the drawer," she said to me. "He turned, and when he saw me with the gun, he shot at me. Not a good shot. I shot back, and luckily, I hit him."

CHAPTER THIRTY-SIX

As I'd figured, Sherman's wound, while serious, was not critical. He was taken to the emergency room, then on to surgery, and then into a room with a 24 hour police guard outside the door.

As soon as he was well enough, he was arraigned and charged with the attempted homicide of Rose. That was just for starters.

Because in the next weeks, the police went after him for the Levy, Clayton and Kohn deaths.

Sherman was a broken man. Even with his attorney, Kenneth McGuire at his side, urging otherwise, Sherman gave it all up.

On Kohn, he said they had another heated argument. During it, Kohn drew out that Smith & Wesson...they wrestled over it...a couple of shots were fired...killing Kohn. Sherman said it was accidental, but he was worried that the way it looked, he'd be charged with murder. So he covered his tracks by taking Kohn's wallet and watch...thus setting up the robbery scene. And he had his wife lie for him, by saying he'd been at home that evening.

Sherman said that Levy knew what had happened with Kohn. Sherman had shared the information with him. And Levy, who – like the others –was grateful for what Sherman had done for all of them in helping them to survive Auschwitz –kept that secret – until his dementia started bringing back memories of the Kohn killing.

Sherman also said it was his idea to have Levy killed. He was worried that Levy, in his dementia-induced ramblings, might come out with the truth about the Kohn killing. Sherman said neither Binder nor Freid knew anything about this. Sherman paid Nesbitt to do the killing, and Clayton to falsify the death certificate.

Sherman claimed he had nothing to do with the hit and run death of Clayton. He did admit that he made two payments to Clayton –the second one being when Clayton threatened to expose him. He couldn't understand how Clayton could make such a threat, because it would also implicate the doctor, himself. But he reported that when Clayton made that claim for the second $5K, he was drunk. Sherman said he figured that Nesbitt decided... on his own...to kill Clayton via the hit and run, because he was worried about Clayton's drinking and then confessing.

One final point on Sherman.

110

While he was under medical care for his wound, one of his sharper doctors thought he spotted something, so he ordered some tests. The results came back, indicating that Sherman was in the early stages of dementia. And although no one could be certain about it, I figured that this might explain why Sherman's behavior had become so erratic.

And why, for example, he'd lost control and tried to confront me in front of the television camera, when he came out from the meeting with Charlie at police headquarters.

As his friend, Ben Binder put it, Sherman was "very agitated ...very upset."

With the height of his irritation being his trying to confront and shoot me in my office.

Dementia, and the roiling of thoughts and actions that come with it. That's what Abe Levy was suffering from, and that's why Sherman had him killed.

And now Sherman, in the early stages of his own dementia, had wanted to kill me.

Sad. Very sad.

As for Edwin Nesbitt, the police caught up with him a couple of weeks later, in Chicago, where he'd started working in another assisted living home. Again, a small one – not one of the chain outfits. I guess it was easier for him to falsify his background.

Nesbitt was brought back to Los Angeles and charged with the murders of Abe Levy and Dr. Clayton. He's in jail, no chance of bail, as the district attorney figures out how to proceed.

Binder and Freid were not charged with anything. As the D.A. put it, their only crime had been one of omission. Back in 1961, they had omitting telling the police that Sherman had asked them not to say anything about the arguments he and Kohn were having. Given their ages, and especially Binder's poor health, it didn't make sense to pursue anything further with either of them.

I wanted to talk to Dr. Clayton's wife, to answer any questions she might have had, but she'd not left a forwarding address. I'm sure that between the computer capabilities of Lu and Rose, we could have located her. But the lady seemed to want to leave all of this behind. And I couldn't blame her. She'd stood by her man right up to his end –although he sure didn't deserve it. Enough. I could only wish her well.

One of the tougher meetings I had, was with Ally Morris. How do you explain to a loving granddaughter, that her grandfather had wrongly kept quiet about how Sherman had stage managed Richard Kohn's death, to make it look like a robbery? About the best that I could do, was to point out a few things to her. First, that Abe Levy was, at best, just an accessory, as regards the death of Richard Kohn. And even that was a stretch.

Second, say what you will, there is no denying that – like Binder and Freid – her grandfather's actions were dominated by the loyalty that he had to Irving Sherman. Could she really fault her grandfather on that score? When he believed that he owed Sherman for his very life and existence at Auschwitz?

Then, there are the folks at the retirement home – Vistas.

As I'd promised Ed Dworsky, I managed to keep the Vistas name at a minimum with the press. Dworsky was one of the good ones, so I was glad I could do so.

And then there was Polly Gladstein, whom Rose called the Yenta of Vistas. I sent Polly a great big bouquet of roses. After all, it was her remembering those names – Semanski, Fedorov, Beletesky and Levenbuk – along with their pictures –that got me started down the right investigative path.

And finally there's the real hero in all of this. Rose Shapiro, my secretary-telephone operator-receptionist-book keeper-Jewish mother-person.

For several weeks after she shot Irving Sherman, the press kept referring to Rose as a Pistol Packin' Grandma.

And some Hollywood producer called her and said he wanted to option the story of her life.

Rose dismissed him with one word – shlimazel – and hung up.

"What'd you say to him?" I asked her.

"A shlimazel. A loser."

Rose looked at me, her face sad.

"Will, to shoot someone is awful. When I shot Sherman, I got a terrible feeling. I never, ever want to have that feeling again."

#

ABOUT THE AUTHOR

After careers as a broadcast journalist and then a public relations counselor, Saul Warshaw, at age 85, now is enjoying his third career—as a writer of mystery thrillers, featuring Will Jonas, a private investigator and former homicide detective with the Los Angeles Police department. Saul and his wife, both native New Yorkers, are longtime residents of Los Angeles. If you wish, please write Saul Warshaw at: saul1warshaw@gmail.com

www.ingramcontent.com/pod-product-compliance
Lightning Source LLC
Chambersburg PA
CBHW051245250626

47155CB00009B/3168